Shattered Illusions

by Lynne Jordan

PublishAmerica
Baltimore

© 2007 by Lynne Jordan.
All rights reserved. No part of this book may be reproduced, stored in a retrieval system or transmitted in any form or by any means without the prior written permission of the publishers, except by a reviewer who may quote brief passages in a review to be printed in a newspaper, magazine or journal.

First printing

All characters in this book are fictitious, and any resemblance to real persons, living or dead, is coincidental.

PublishAmerica has allowed this work to remain exactly as the author intended, verbatim, without editorial input.

ISBN: 1-60441-925-3
PUBLISHED BY PUBLISHAMERICA, LLLP
www.publishamerica.com
Baltimore

Printed in the United States of America

Thank you to my parents for always being there for me, my sister for making sure I could stand up for myself, and to my husband for always allowing me to be myself.

Thank you for believing in me.

Prologue

Pineville, Minnesota, 1979

She was dead. Just like that, Ray McMillan became a widower at thirty. A single father left to raise his two-year-old daughter alone.

A drunk driver had taken Veronica, the woman he'd loved since high school, from him three days ago. At least she hadn't had a chance to realize it was happening. The coroner had said she'd been killed instantly. Sure, the driver was in jail, and would most likely be convicted of vehicular manslaughter and go to prison someday, but that didn't give Ray back his wife. It didn't give his little girl back her mother.

Janine. What was he going to do about her? He was all she had left. He was solely responsible for providing her with everything she would ever need, and how was he going to manage that with all the debt that now lay on his shoulders? They had a huge mortgage on the house they'd bought only three years ago, car payments, credit cards, old pregnancy expenses, and all the typical bills married couples accumulate. The problem was that he was no longer part of a married couple. He had to pay all of that off by himself. It was impossible. There hadn't been a life insurance policy. Veronica was only twenty-seven. She wasn't supposed to die.

Panicking, Ray raked his fingers through his sandy brown hair. He saw his red-rimmed, sorrow-filled blue eyes staring back at him out of the glass on the counter next to the cash register. What was he doing at work, anyway? He'd only buried his wife yesterday. He looked around at McMillan Booksellers, the bookstore that had been passed down to him all the way from his grandfather.

It was a beautiful shop, a haven for intellectuals. Books surrounded him, placed neatly in floor-to-ceiling shelves all the way around the store: old books, new ones, rare books, and cheap ones, the educational and the entertaining. McMillan Booksellers had them all. Regal burgundy drapery covered the high, arching windows, and oak hardwood floor lead to a staircase that curved gracefully up to the second level. A deep brown leather couch and two recliners faced a marble fireplace in the lobby, inviting anyone to cozy up with a book and a non-alcoholic beverage of choice, and drift away from their reality. His grandfather had known exactly how to achieve the ambience needed for comfort.

If only Ray could drift away from his reality.

He had to sell it. It broke his heart to be the one to destroy the family legacy, but he had no other choice. He had a little girl to take care of. The income he brought in from the business wouldn't even make a dent in the mounds of debt that now faced him. If he sold it, he could get at least enough money to pay off the house. Who knows what he would do from there? He didn't have any other skills. He'd worked at the bookstore since he was fifteen years old. There had never been another career option for him.

He had no choice. Resigned, he picked up his stack of mail. An envelope with no return address caught his eye. It lay on top of the pile of bills and almost seemed to call to him. Curious, he opened it with his antique letter opener.

As he read past the sympathies, his eyes opened wide. He felt a bud of hope blooming. This was an opportunity he couldn't miss. Sure, it was illegal, but it would only be for the short term. All he had to do was make a few deliveries, stock provided, and he'd have enough money to pay off the house and keep the bookstore open. Plus, this Xavier was offering a bonus of ten thousand dollars to start! All he had to do was call and ask for specific instructions. It was brilliant.

Imagine using a bookstore as a front for delivering cocaine. Who'd have thought of that? Who would ever suspect? Ray smiled to himself. Xavier had been doing it for ten years already, and he'd never gotten caught. As long as Ray was just as careful, he wouldn't either.

Besides, it was only for a little while. Just long enough to pay off his debts, maybe set aside enough money for Janine to go to college someday...

"Xavier, you're my savior," he said aloud. Then, picking up the phone, he agreed, unaware that he had just signed his life away.

Chapter One

Bass Lake, Minnesota, 1987

"Dad, look! I caught a fish!" Beaming, Janine McMillan, now ten years old, held up her pole, and, sure enough, a crappie wriggled at the end of it.

"Way to go, kiddo!" Ray exclaimed. "It's a keeper, too. Get it in here, I'll take it off the hook."

"No, I want to," Janine stated, excited to try her hand at a new task. She flopped the fish onto the floor of their fishing boat, and stepped on it with her pink sandaled foot. Bending over, she gingerly touched the slimy body, and began prying the hook out of its mouth.

Ray watched her work at it, with her tongue sticking out the side of her mouth, and grinned. She was beautiful, his little girl. He'd done well so far. She was smart, happy, and, fortunately for her, had been too young when her mother died to have the scars on her heart.

It was too bad Janine had never really known Veronica. They were so similar. Her blonde hair was stick-straight like her mother's had been, though lighter than Veronica's strawberry blonde, and currently pulled back into the braided pigtails he'd finally mastered. She had her mother's brown eyes, and his poor vision. He liked the way his daughter looked in her little pink-framed glasses, studious, and older somehow. How she'd gotten to be ten years old already was beyond him. Time flew.

Janine finally got the hook loose, and picked up the fish. He held the fish basket out to her just as she dropped it. The crappie smacked onto the blue lid, and fell in.

"Ouch! The fish bit me," Janine said, frowning and holding up her thumb, where a small bubble of blood was forming.

"Fish don't bite, sweetheart. He must have stuck you with his fin," Ray tossed the basket over the side of the boat and reached for the dishtowel he kept close at hand. He pressed down on the wound for a minute, checked to see if the bleeding had stopped, and kissed it all better for her.

"Thanks, Daddy." Happy again, Janine bounced back into her seat and stuck another worm on her hook. Clumsily, she cast with all her might. The bobber landed with a plop in the water a few feet away from the boat.

"Nice cast, Neeny. You're becoming a pro already." She was doing well for her first time out. Why Ray had never taken the time to teach her how to fish was beyond him. He kicked back in his seat, placed his feet on the side of the boat, and cast his own line out. Tipping his head back, he enjoyed the sensation of the July sun beating down on his face. Fishing was so relaxing. He needed to make more time for it in the future. "Catch a few more and I'll teach you how to clean them tonight," Ray promised.

"I have to clean them?" Janine asked, confused. "Don't they live in the water?" Her eyebrows crinkled the way her mother's used to when asking a serious question.

After a stupefied moment, Ray laughed. "No, honey, the fish don't need a bath. You clean them so we can eat them. It means clean out the bones and the scales."

"Ewww! I don't wanna do that! That's gross." Janine's expression was so filled with disgust, that Ray had to laugh again.

"All right, I'll do it this time, and you can watch. We'll have a fish fry for supper." Ray smiled as Janine, looking relieved, turned her concentration back to her Snoopy bobber. Seeing his own bobber go under, he reeled in, effortlessly slapped another crappie into the fish basket, and let his mind drift.

Business was booming at the bookstore, both legal, and illegal. He supposed he hadn't made the time to bring her out before. He'd been too busy providing for her financially. That letter from Xavier, whom he still had never met, had been a lifesaver so many years ago. He'd not only managed to save the money needed to pay off all his debts, but also to put aside enough for Janine to go to college and have a decent trust fund afterward. He also had a nice little numbered account with plenty in it for his own retirement.

He'd been careful with what he'd done with the money. He had several numbered accounts at a bank in Switzerland. One of those contained the money it would take to pay off the debts, but he was smart enough to continue making monthly payments. He'd also made sure that his reported income increased subtly but steadily every year. If he needed more money than that, he had an emergency stash of cash. He couldn't afford to attract attention. He'd gotten away with this for eight years so far, but he wanted to be done with it. He was terrified more and more each year that his daughter would somehow find out what he was up to. He had no idea how he'd explain that.

Besides, he was a decent man. He wasn't a drug dealer at heart, and couldn't continue to be one because it was against his own morals. He had all the money he would need for the rest of his and Janine's lives. There was no reason to continue doing this. The longer he kept it up, the more likely he was to get caught. He'd have to give Xavier a call when they returned home and give his resignation.

For now, he was going to enjoy a beautiful afternoon with his daughter.

They fished until the mosquitoes came out and scared them away. They had gotten quite a haul, and Janine watched in horrified awe as he began to slice through the scales below the first fish's head.

"Won't that kill him, Daddy?" she asked.

"Well, you can't eat live fish, sweetie. Don't worry. It doesn't hurt them for long. Besides, before you know it, they'll look just like the fish we buy at the store."

"Ohh…" fascinated now, Janine continued to watch. By the time they got to the last one, she was itching to try it herself. "Let me, Daddy! Let me!"

"Are you sure? I thought it was gross. You'll get fish guts all over you."

"But it has to be done so we can survive out here." Her voice was so melodramatic that his mouth twitched.

"That's right. Be careful so you don't cut yourself, now."

Janine nodded and got to work, tongue poking out again. Ray felt pride rushing through him as she mangled her way through the fish.

"With a little work, you'll be a fish cleaning queen."

Janine smiled proudly as she held up the remains of the fish. Ray clapped for her, and bowed. She laughed. He took a quick picture to remember the occasion.

"You're growing up on me, Neeny. Now that you know how to survive out here, you'll probably be moving out on me."

She giggled. "No, I won't, daddy. I'll never move out." She threw her arms around him, fish scales and all. Ray felt a pang, knowing that someday she would. With a quick pat on the back, he instructed her to throw the fish parts away and barely caught her before she took the bowl of meat as well.

Ray spent the next half hour helping her build a fire, and showing her how to make the beer batter. Seconds later, the fish were sizzling on the grill, and a tantalizing aroma filled the air. They ate their catch and enjoyed each other's company as the sun dropped beneath the distant horizon. Supper aside, they told ghost stories. It had been a long time since Ray had spent this much time with his daughter outside of the bookstore. He was glad he'd taken this opportunity.

Worn out from chasing each other around, they sat back to watch the fireworks display shooting up from the distant shores of Bass Lake.

After the fireworks faded, leaving ghostly trails behind them in the black sky, Janine fell strangely quiet. She raised her head up from her father's shoulder, and looked straight at him. "What was Mommy like?"

Ray felt as if she'd kicked him in the stomach. She'd asked about her mother before, of course, but never with that serious note in her voice. Ray cleared his throat and turned to face her. "She was beautiful."

You look a lot like her. She loved doing this kind of thing, camping, fishing. I guess that's probably another reason why I haven't taken you to do these things before."

"Did you love her?"

"Oh, yes. I loved your mother very much. She was always there for me, never let me down. She made me happy." Feeling his throat tighten, he gathered close what his wife had left him and hugged her tight. "You sound like her when you laugh."

"Really?" Janine smiled. "Do I make you happy, too?"

"Of course you do! I don't know what I'd do without you." He ruffled her hair.

"Did you meet mom in school?"

"As a matter of fact, I did. High school. We played the saxophone in the band together. I thought she was cute, so I asked her out. We got along really well, and before we knew it, we loved each other. Next thing we knew, we were married, and having you." He tugged her onto his lap. "She loved you so much. I'd never seen her more happy than the day she had you. You had fuzzy blond hair just like hers. She called you her precious angel."

"And now she's my precious angel," Janine said quietly, looking suddenly very grown up. "She watches over me from up in heaven, and I'll always have her in my heart." Tears welled up in her brown eyes. "But I can't talk to her, Dad."

Ray fought back his own tears, and kissed the top of her head. "You can talk to her, she just can't answer you."

"But I want her to answer me."

"You can talk to me, and I can answer you."

She turned her face to his with a speculative look. "Can I talk to you about things, like my friends do with their mothers?"

Uneasy, Ray worried that she wanted to talk about sex. After reminding himself that she was only ten, he answered her cautiously. "Like what?"

"Well..." Janine twirled one of her braids around. She glanced at him hesitantly a couple of times, and took a deep breath. "I like this boy from school," she said quickly, "and he's not very nice to me. He pulls my hair and throws things at the back of my head in class. And now, cuz it's summer, he follows me around on his bike all the time and calls me four-eyes."

Ray felt relief flood through him. Thank God. He'd be able to avoid that sticky subject at least a little longer. He settled himself against a log and prepared to rant and rave about how nasty little boys could be. He reassured his daughter that all this boy's teasing probably meant he liked her, too. But, of course, he added that she would have to wait until she was at least fifteen to date this boy. That was being reasonable. He'd really have liked to tell her she had to wait until she was fifty.

Crisis averted, and wanting to put a smile back on her face, he tickled her until happy tears replaced the sad ones.

Gasping with laughter, Janine broke free of his grasp and threw her arms around her father. "You're the best daddy in the world!"

He hugged her tightly, glad to hear it. "You're the best daughter in the world."

They returned home a few nights later, and Ray tucked Janine into bed. He kissed her good night, and closed the bedroom door behind him. He walked downstairs to the kitchen and over to the phone. Picking it up, he dialed the number he'd been ordered to memorize and destroy eight years ago.

He felt the chill that always accompanied these calls when Xavier answered. He had always told himself he felt that way because of the voice distorter Xavier used on the line. It had never struck him as odd. After all, the man was a drug dealer. He wouldn't want anyone recognizing his voice.

"Xavier, it's Ray."

"Well, hello, Ray. Did you enjoy your camping trip?" The voice gurgled.

For a moment, Ray didn't know how the man had known he'd been camping, then figured he must have told him at some point. Or at least one of the employees they shared. "Yes, I did. Very much, thanks."

"What can I do for you?"

"I want out, Xavier." He found it hard to control a slight tremor in his voice. Why was he afraid?

"Excuse me?" the voice rattled.

"I want out." Ray repeated, without the tremor.

"Do you think that's wise, Ray?"

"Yes. I've made enough to pay off all my debts, and for Janine's college. I don't need to do this anymore, and I'd rather not."

"Oh, you'd rather not?" Xavier repeated. Even through the voice distorter, Ray could hear the ice in the voice. He began to shake.

"No."

"You don't have a choice, young man. You're in this too deep already. I can't afford to let you leave now."

Young man? He was thirty-eight years old, for Pete's sake. "I'm afraid I have to, Xavier, for my daughter's sake. I swear I won't tell anyone about the business."

"I'm afraid, for your daughter's sake, you'll have to stay in the business."

"Are you threatening me?"

"I don't make threats, Raymond. I make promises. Get this silly idea out of your head, or you and your daughter will come to harm. This is not the kind of business you can just walk away from when you've made enough money. I have clients to provide for, and I can't do that without your help. Do you understand?"

"I'm out. That's final." A drop of sweat dribbled down Ray's back. He was ice cold.

"That's not a wise move." Xavier grumbled.

"That's the one I'm making. You leave my daughter out of this, or I swear I'll turn your whole operation over to the police." Ray shouted into the phone, his grip like a vice on the receiver. He slammed the phone down so fiercely, that he knocked it off the wall mount. He stood there, shaking with anger and an inkling of fear. He poured himself a shot of whiskey, and slept on the couch near the front door just in case.

When Ray stepped outside to grab the newspaper the next morning, he found a stray cat lying on the rug in front of the door, its throat slashed. Pinned to it was a note:

Your daughter could be next. There's no "out." There's just dead.

Oh shit. Shit. What had he gotten himself into? Trembling with bone-deep fear, he did his best to scrape up the mess before his daughter could see it. There was nothing he could do. He had gotten himself stuck with a crazy man for the rest of his life. He'd just have to make damn sure his daughter never found out.

Chapter Two

Pineville, Minnesota, 2005

Janine hummed happily to herself as she strode down the familiar, tree-lined street to McMillan Booksellers. Hardly even needing to glance up to see where she was going, she paged through the brochure the florist had given her. Even though her wedding was only three months away, she still could hardly believe she was actually getting married.

Smiling up at the sun-drenched, turquoise June sky, she tossed her waist-length blond hair over her shoulder and adjusted the book bag she carried. Her deep brown eyes misted over, as they so often did lately, as she thought of how incredibly lucky she was.

Brian Whitman was the man of her dreams. Two years older than her own twenty-eight, he was honest, loving, intelligent, funny, and absolutely adored her. Plus he was gorgeous and unbelievably tender in bed. Janine felt a flush creeping across her cheeks as she thought it. Well, he was.

She had met him four years ago when he had started working with her father at the bookstore. It had been the summer before she'd gone back to Harvard for her third degree. They'd danced around each other that first month, both being shy, and each of them secretly attracted to the other. At her father's encouragement, Janine had finally asked him out. She suspected that even then, her father had known that they would someday be married.

She had been delighted when she discovered that Brian shared her fascination with the written word. They had discussed the varied works of Shakespeare, Emily Dickinson, T.S. Eliot, and J.R.R. Tolkien over pizza on their first date. Brian had confessed his secret ambition of being a writer, and she had encouraged him, though nothing had ever come of it. She quickly figured out that Brian was perfectly content living off his trust fund and lacked ambition, but she had long ago been able to overlook that slightly irritating flaw. Both of his parents were stockbrokers, and his trust fund was large enough to keep him extremely comfortable for the whole of his natural life.

Janine could certainly relate. The trust fund her mother had left her was nearly as substantial. Her mother's money had already paid for Harvard for the eight years Janine had attended, and that had hardly made a dent in it. At least she had degrees in Literature, Accounting, and Foreign Languages to show for it. Brian didn't even have one degree. Most people at least had one in this day and age.

Janine would be the first to admit that she had gone a little nuts with her own education, especially when she simply intended to run her father's bookstore. She just really enjoyed learning new things. The foreign languages degree was a bonus to help her be better able to communicate with the wide range of cultures that were rapidly appearing in Minnesota, as in the rest of the United States. Besides, the majority of her father's employees spoke Spanish. Ray McMillan was the kind of man who encouraged the minorities in their quests to make better lives.

Wow. How had her mind run off on that tangent? Back to Brian. She smiled again as she remembered what their relationship had been like back then. For the first two years, they had seen each other only when Janine had come home from school, and on a couple of occasions in which Brian had come to visit her in the dorms. When she'd finally finished school, just last year, their relationship had really blossomed. Within two months of her return, Brian had proposed to her over a romantic candlelit dinner at his house. She had moved in with him immediately.

Janine held out her left hand, and watched the two-carat princess-cut diamond cast rainbows in the sunlight. She smiled, sighed happily, and turned her gaze back to her brochure.

The one thing she loved most about Brian was how much like her father he was.

In her mind, Ray McMillan was the greatest man on earth. He had been the perfect father the entire time she'd been growing up. He had never raised a hand to her, and had supported her in everything she'd done. When teenage boys had broken her heart, her father had been there to hold her while she cried, and to eat ice cream with her while she healed. He'd written to her and called her regularly while she was in college, and had welcomed her home with pizza and some fantastic gift at the end of every year. He had been bursting with pride each time she'd earned a degree.

He'd bought her first car, and had replaced it with hardly even a lecture when she'd totaled it in an accident. He'd been so happy that she hadn't been hurt, that he had bought her a new one the very next day. He'd given her a credit card that he paid off every month so that she could buy all the clothes she wanted. He had taught her to respect all people, to be honest and caring, and had given her confidence. Above all, he had showered her with love. Janine considered herself lucky that her best friend was her father.

Now she had Brian as well. Not every girl was fortunate enough to have two such wonderful men in her life.

Because her father had helped her plan everything that had to do with her wedding even more than Brian had, she was excited to hear his opinion on the flowers she was leaning toward. She paused at the foot of the steps leading up to the bookstore and admired the view for a moment.

McMillan Booksellers, established in 1910, was a weathered brown brick building, covered with ivy, identical to most of the buildings on Main Street. Unlike the others, it lay twenty feet off the road, flanked by a beautifully landscaped hill, and guarded by a white picket fence. The yard was bedecked with tall, stately oak and elm trees, and an abundance of flowers and shade to give it more of a homey than businesslike appearance. The focal point of its decorative surroundings was a rose garden in full bloom. This Eden could only be reached by passing under an old white arbor draped with a rainbow of climbing roses. Should the sheer beauty of this haven overcome the visitor, lacy stone benches were set strategically along the cobblestone path. Janine had sat upon those benches, curled up with Anne of Green Gables or Jane Eyre, blocking out civilization many times in her youth.

The beauty of the yard drew the visitor's eye away from the fenced-off, ugly gravel alleyway that led to the shipping and receiving door at the back of the building. The flowers that bordered the stone staircase widened and leaned over the path as they drew closer to the double doors at the top, as if the blooms themselves were clamoring to get inside and be swept away by the adventures of Tom Sawyer and Huckleberry Finn.

Janine swept up the stairs and pushed open the door to what sometimes seemed like her second home. Her humming changed to match the strains of Mozart that flowed out of hidden speakers. She breathed in deeply and air redolent of books, leather, and gourmet coffee caressed her senses. The interior of the bookstore could have been the library of a wealthy book fanatic with its burgundy fabrics and brown leather furniture.

She glanced around the shop for her father, but didn't see him. With a wave to Juan, one of the few English-speaking employees, who manned the antique register, and entering the code, she headed into the back room.

Here, all essence of beauty fled. The floors were concrete, and the walls cement blocks. The only landscaping was in the forms of hundreds of palettes of plastic-wrapped books. The temperature was considerably cooler, so that Janine felt goose bumps rise to dance along her arms. What struck her as most unusual was the complete silence. Normally, the music from the shop could be heard in here as well, especially if her father was doing inventory as he so often was. Business was always booming at the bookstore.

Glancing at her watch, and noting that it was almost three o'clock, she confirmed her thought that it was too late for her father to be on lunch break. Curious about where he might be, she looked around for a few minutes. Planning to come back later, she turned to go, and bumped squarely into a half-unwrapped palette of books, knocking a few copies of Webster's Dictionary to the ground.

Rubbing her bruised arm, she bent to pick them up. Suddenly, she stopped.

"What's this?" she asked the empty room. One of the books had opened and fallen face down. A small plastic bag filled with white powder had fallen out. Picking up both the bag and the book, she noticed a cutout in the middle pages, right in the center of the 'M' section. A peculiar chill washed over her. Could this be what she thought it was?

"Cocaine," she whispered. It was just a guess based on several movies she'd seen in the past, but something told her it was right. "It can't be!" She was unnerved by the shrill sound of her own voice. What did this mean? Surely her father couldn't have known about this. Although she knew it was stereotypical, her mind immediately jumped to the dozens of Latino employees her father had hired. Then it took an odd twist. What if those employees were all illegal aliens that her father knew would keep his secret over the threat of being deported? Or worse?

"No." she whispered. But once again, something told her she was right.

Her heart pounding, she shoved the packet back in the book, closed it, and raced out the back door. Since her father wasn't around, she had to talk to Brian. Tears misted her deep brown eyes again, but this time they stemmed from a bone-deep despair that she might have been wrong about the man who had raised her.

She turned out of the alley, and headed back the way she had come. Brian's house was only a few blocks away from the store. He'd bought it for convenience. She knew he'd be home. She'd just talked to him on her cell when she'd been at the florist's. She dashed down the street, unaware that she was being watched from a silver Ford Mustang on the other side of the road.

Her bag struck her back roughly, and remembering that her laptop was in it, she slowed her pace. She took a few deep breaths, trying to calm her speeding heart. She didn't know anything for sure, she told herself. There had to be a rational explanation that did not turn her father, her best friend, into a drug dealer. But she couldn't think of one. She dashed up the steps to the house she shared with Brian and shoved open the door.

Brian glanced up from his book and smiled as she burst in the door. She looked beautiful today, he thought as he admired the flat black sandals and short black denim shorts that showed off miles of slender, tanned legs. The red tank top gathered between her breasts, enhancing the small swell and drawing the eyes just there. The pendant of the three-stone diamond necklace he'd given her for their second anniversary twinkled and flashed in the sunshine that filtered through the sheer shades on the windows. Her long hair fell over her shoulders and across her back in a curtain of gold fire. All five foot, ten inches of her was stunning, though lacking in curves. She belonged in sunny California, not Minnesota. Brian's gaze swept over her in an instant, and his smile faded when she whipped off her sunglasses, revealing tear-drenched eyes and a grief-ravaged face.

"Oh, baby," he was off the couch and holding her in his arms in a second. "What's wrong?" he asked her as she began to cry harder, heart-wrenching sobs that convulsed her whole upper torso. She clung to him as though he was a life raft and she was drowning in a sea of anguish. He rubbed her back, shushed her, and waited for the torrent of tears to subside so she could speak again. "What's wrong, Neeny? Talk to me."

Finally, her breathing returned almost to normal, though punctuated with hiccups. She lifted her tear-stained eyes to him and gazed into the face she had fallen in love with. Brown eyes darker than hers, filled with concern; wavy brown hair falling over strong, worry-wrinkled eyebrows; and a narrow, unblemished face with a rounded chin looked down at her. He stood a mere three inches above her. His strong, lean arms were banded around her, hers around his narrow waist. She tucked her head on his shoulder a moment, to regain her calm, and pulled back. Wiping her eyes with the handkerchief he'd given her, she handed him the book.

"A dictionary?" He was confused. "You're crying about a dictionary? What? Did you look up a word and realize you'd been using it incorrectly?" His effort at cheering her up only rewarded him with a nasty look.

"Open it," she suggested, crossing her arms in front of her chest.

He obliged her with a roll of his eyes. When he saw the packet inside, his face went carefully blank. He tossed it on an end table and looked at her.

Janine felt a fresher, fiercer stab of betrayal. Only this time, it was anger that filled her. Her voice dangerously low, she asked the question. "Did you know about this?"

"I found out a couple years ago, before you finished school. He didn't want you to know."

She could feel him drawing away from her. "Who didn't? My father? How long has he been doing this?"

Brian sat back down on the couch, and put his head in his hands. He had a feeling she was going to leave him for this. "He's been doing this since your mom died. He told me it was for your own good, and that you could never find out."

Shocked, Janine sank back onto the arm of a recliner behind her. Barely able to speak, she answered. "Since my mom died?" Brian nodded. Furious, she sprang back up. "My mother never left me a trust fund, did she?" He shook his head. "So everything he's ever bought for me, my college…*everything*! It was drug money. *Oooh!* I can't believe that bastard lied to me about everything in my entire life!" Eyes blazing, wishing she could throw something and watch it shatter into a million pieces, she turned on Brian. "And *you*! You did it, too. Two big, brave, stupid men supporting the little woman with drug money!" She whipped off her ring. "I suppose you bought *this* with your drug money, too!"

Brian jumped to his feet, hands raised as if to fend off an attack. "No!" He shouted. "Janine, I was never a part of that business! I just knew about it. God, please don't think that about me! I *love* you!"

She stomped up and shoved her finger within an inch of his face. He winced. He'd never seen her so angry. "How do I know that?

How can you expect me to believe anything you've ever said to me? You've lied to me for *four years!*"

"Two," he interjected, then flinched when she raised her arm as if to slap him.

With deliberate control, she lowered her arm. "Two years," she growled, "is not in any way better. By not telling me, you *lied* to me. I can never trust you again. You know that there is nothing in this world more important to me than honesty." She stepped back, sobs hitching in her chest again. She looked at the ring, looked at Brian, and set it on the end table on top of the dictionary. "The wedding is off." The tears spilled over. "I *never* want to see you again," she told him vehemently.

She took one last look at him, but now, instead of handsome, he just looked weak. Weak and pathetic. She picked up her discarded book bag, and turned toward the door.

"Janine...please," Brian begged her, grabbing her arm, "I love you. I'm sorry I lied to you, and I'll never do it again. I promise. Please don't leave me." Tears misted his eyes, trembled in his voice.

She stopped, lowered her angry gaze to his hand, and brushed it off as if the very thought of his touch disgusted her. "If you loved me, you never would have done this. Goodbye, Brian." With that, she sailed out the door, slamming it behind her, oblivious to the sobbing she heard in her wake.

She'd hardened her heart to him now, and her father. But before she left, she was going to give her father a piece of her mind. With rage brewing inside her, she stormed back to the bookstore. He'd just better be there this time.

Juan blinked when he saw her come back in the shop. He hadn't seen her leave, and this abrupt change surprised him. When she'd entered before, she'd been grinning ear to ear. Now she looked like a woman both capable and willing to kill someone. He saw where she was heading, and jumped to defend his employer's secret. "*Senorita* McMillan, ju can't go back there!!" He called. "Ju *must not* go back there!" He started after her.

Janine, ignoring Juan, started to slam the door to the storeroom, but heard her father's angry voice, and closed it quietly behind her.

"I don't *care* if Jose says he didn't go to the police. Xavier *knows* he did." Ray McMillan spoke in fluent Spanish.

Janine grimaced at the anger and underlying terror in her father's voice. Who was Xavier? She crept closer. She gasped when she saw her father holding a gun on two of his employees.

"Now you two find him, and *take care of him*." Despite his respectable business suit, her father directed them to the door with his gun as if he were the Godfather himself. They backed away, nodding and looking frightened. "You know the rules. Make it look like suicide, or Xavier will have your heads."

A small scream escaped Janine as the implications of her father's Spanish words struck home. Just then, Juan opened the door behind her. Her father's blue eyes filled with horror as they connected with hers.

"Grab her!" He ordered Juan, in English. "Neeny, let me explain!"

She wasn't waiting around for any explanations. She plowed her elbow into Juan's stomach as he grabbed her, stomped on his instep, and kicked him square between the legs. He fell to the ground. Janine leapt over his prone form like a gazelle, desperate to escape the man that used to be the father she loved. She heard him calling out to her. Giving him a piece of her mind had fallen way down on her priority list. Now she knew her first and only priority was to stay alive.

She ran out the door, heedless to her father's pleading cries, and the banging of her bag against her back. Not only was he a drug dealer, now she knew that he was a murderer as well. Sobs threatened to consume her as she plowed through the double doors. She missed a step, and stumbled, but quickly regained her balance, long legs eating up the ground beneath her. She vaulted over the picket fence and sprinted toward town, trying to ignore her father's voice fading behind her.

She heard a screech, and glanced up to see a silver Ford Mustang pull to the curb. The passenger door burst open, and a man leaned out.

That's my favorite car, she thought irrationally, as she swung over to avoid the gunshots she was sure would follow.

"Get in!" a gruff voice called from the car. She hesitated for an instant, saw the gold flash of a police badge, and jumped in.

The man careened away from the curb and plowed down the road, heading out of town. She glanced over her shoulder in time to see her father, her best friend, fall to his knees. His big hands covered his face, the sun glinting off of the gun he still held, and instinctively, Janine knew that he was crying for the daughter he knew he'd just lost.

Grieving for her shattered illusions.

Chapter Three

"This is my favorite car," Janine told the man numbly.

"Thanks. Mine, too. Just got it a few months ago," he glanced at her. She sure was a sight. Long legs in short clothes, gorgeous hair he'd love to get his hands on. He enjoyed a brief fantasy involving chocolate syrup and tan legs, then shook himself. Jesus. What was he thinking? He didn't even know her name. For all he knew, she could be a coke whore who had just pissed off the wrong supplier. She didn't look like one, though. She looked like a wholesome, healthy, All-American California girl: the kind with no brain that popped huge wads of bubble gum in their mouths and said 'like' a lot. Her comment about his car only enhanced his opinion. "You okay?"

He almost drove off the road when she burst into tears. He patted her fruitlessly while she sobbed. He hated tears. Nothing hurt a man's heart like the sound of a woman crying. And this woman kept it up all the way into Minneapolis. Twenty straight minutes of weeping had his nerves unraveling like a badly woven rug. He pulled into the police station and all but leaped out of his car, with a sharp order for her to stay put.

He opened the door to the station, and reveled in the relative silence for a moment. Purposefully, he strode across the office in which a cacophony of ringing telephones, clacking keyboards, and chattering voices converged into familiar, soothing music. He slapped into the captain's office and plopped himself on the leather chair, settling his feet on the desk in a pose that mirrored his superior's.

Captain Krista Mulroney, short and stout, glared at him from piercing blue eyes like an angry dwarf. Her short black hair sat on her head like a helmet, and gave the impression of a dwarven general on the warpath. "Get your feet off my desk, Turner."

Craig obliged, sitting up straight and grinning at her like a kid caught with his hand in the cookie jar. "Picked me up a potential witness in the McMillan case, Cap'n."

"You're on suspension, Detective. Need I remind you that you aren't supposed to be investigating anything on your own?" Captain Mulroney stood up, glaring ferociously, then grinned. "Welcome back, Turner." She opened her desk, tossed him his police-issue Colt .45 and his badge, and shook his hand. "Who did you nab?"

Craig tucked the badge into his pocket, right on top of the spare he'd kept at home. "I haven't gotten that far. She's currently sobbing her brains out in my Mustang."

"So, how do you know she's a potential witness?" Krista settled herself back in her chair, and kicked her feet up. She'd known Craig Turner since he was in his early twenties, just starting out. She'd worked with his father before he'd been killed, and although she was only thirteen years older than Craig's thirty-four, she felt slightly maternal toward him.

"Well, considering that I picked her up as she was running for her life away from a gun-toting Ray McMillan himself, I'm pretty sure she is. Plus, that gives us enough for a warrant to search the place." Craig gloated.

Krista smiled at him. "Bring her up, Detective."

"Yes, ma'am," Craig saluted her and headed back to his car to fetch the girl.

To his dismay, she was still crying. He sighed, rolled his eyes, and opened her door. She shrieked and moved away. "C'mon up and meet the captain," he told her.

She sniffled, hiccupped, and looked up at him through terrorized brown eyes. "I'm (hic) not leaving (hic) this car." Janine told him. She knew she was being ridiculous, but she simply couldn't handle any more excitement that day. She crossed her arms and refused to budge.

Craig tried all methods of persuasion, including tugging on her, but she wouldn't move. With an exasperated sigh, he sat back in the driver's seat and took out his cell phone. "Cap'n, she ain't movin'."

"Fine, take her home, then. We'll ask her some questions tomorrow," Krista told him. "At least get her name."

"What's your name?" he asked her grumpily, turning her way.

"Janine McMillan. What's yours?" she asked him just as grumpily.

Craig paused to let his stomach stop flopping with excitement. Janine McMillan, Ray's only child. She could be the person to bring him down. He relayed her name to the captain, smiling at her quick intake of breath.

"Holy cow, Craig," Krista murmured. The tips of her fingers were tingling. "Take good care of that one. Nice grab."

"Thanks. Don't worry, I will." He flipped his phone shut and looked at Janine with renewed interest. She glared at him.

"Do you have a name?" Janine grumbled.

"Yeah," he held out his hand, "I'm Detective Craig Turner, Minneapolis P.D." She shook it, surprising Craig with strength. She was a tough California girl. "Well, let's get you home." He started the car.

"NO!" Janine wailed. Instantly, the waterworks were rolling again. "I can't go home!"

Jeez, wasn't the well empty yet? "Why not?"

"I don't have one anymore." She wiped her face, frustrated that the tears wouldn't stop. "Are you stupid, or did you just not know that my father was chasing me with a gun?"

"Yeah, I knew. You're a little old to still be living with Daddy."

She sniffled again. "I was living with my fiancé, who might also be involved. I'd just dumped him before I went to the bookstore."

"Rough day," Craig commented.

"No kidding, genius," she snapped, bawling again. "I'm (hic) staying with you. That's (hic) final!"

Craig barely stopped a frustrated growl. "The last thing I need on my hands is some blubbering female. It's out of the question." He slapped a hand on the steering wheel to emphasize it. *"That's* final."

"Then I'm not telling you anything." Janine crossed those long legs, crossed her arms, and stared out the window.

That did it. Craig couldn't afford to throw her off a bridge. Unable to stop the growl this time, he flipped open his phone and informed his captain that Janine would be staying with him. He closed it, and stomped on the gas pedal with so much force that the Mustang's tires squealed. Screeching out of the parking lot, he headed to his house.

Lucky for her, he failed to notice Janine's smug look. At least she had control over something that had happened that day.

Silence filled the car on the way to Craig's house. Surreptitiously, Janine studied him. He was very handsome for a grouchy cop. The similarity in appearance between Craig Turner and Brian had tears sneaking up on her again. Craig's hair was a darker brown than Brian's, almost black, and he had eyes to match. He was also badly in need of a haircut. He was much more toughly built than Brian was, a rough and ready sort. Faint lines around his eyes and mouth gave Craig the appearance of a man who'd had his own share of troubles. Despite herself, Janine wondered what had happened in his life. Of course, Brian was a trust-fund baby who'd had it about as easy as it could get. He'd never had to work a day in his life until he'd started at the bookstore out of sheer boredom.

Deliberately, she shifted her thoughts away from Brian, and dared to ask a question that had been on her mind. "What were you doing there?"

"At the bookstore?" Craig asked, turning those dark eyes to hers. She nodded. "Surveillance."

"Why? I mean, how did you know...?" She broke off, still afraid to incriminate her father.

"That something might be going down there?" She nodded again. "We had a call from a potential informant a couple of days ago. He said he wanted to tell us about illegal activities taking place there. We wanted him to come in and make a statement, but he never showed up. Been watching the place since. I have been, anyway, sort of unofficially. I have a special interest in drug busts." Craig clamped down on bitter memories of the night his father was killed during one. None of her business. "Any idea who the caller might have been?"

Janine hesitated. "Someone named Jose, I think. He started working with my father a few months ago. I didn't think he spoke much English. I think a couple of my father's other employees are going to kill him today. That's what Dad was instructing them to do when I walked in. That's how I found out…" She trailed off, her voice breaking again. She rubbed her eyes in frustration. "God! I can't stop *crying*!"

"I noticed." Craig commented. "Any idea where this Jose lives?"

She shook her head, mopping at her face.

"It'll be hard to save him, then. There're probably at least a hundred Jose's around here. Besides, he's probably an illegal alien if he's working for those kinds of people. We'll just have to see what happens next." He called his captain again to give her a heads up anyway. Glancing at Janine when he was through, he felt a stirring of pity. She looked exhausted. She was leaning her head back, her eyes closed. She looked too pale, even for a blond.

A few minutes later, he pulled into his driveway. The little one-story white house barely had room for him, let alone a houseguest.

Janine checked out the scenery as she got out of the car. Obviously, all his money had gone to buy his car. The house was old and badly in need of fresh paint. What looked like dead hydrangeas flanked the single front step, and the flowerbed across the front ran rampant with weeds. Tucked into a small section of forest, the house looked comforting to Janine despite the disrepair. It was barely six o'clock in the evening, and she was ready for bed.

Three hours ago, her life had been normal. She'd been happily planning a wedding that was no longer happening, and had been excited to share it with the father she'd loved. She'd lost her innocence today. Never again would she be so naïve. Never again would she be able to completely trust anyone. Her eyes grew wet again.

Craig heard her sniffle behind him as he unlocked the door. Rolling his eyes skyward, he prayed fervently that he would not have to listen to that all night. He opened the door and let her in.

She surveyed her surroundings with tired eyes. The place was almost without furniture. A frumpy plaid couch sat in the living room, beside a recliner covered in the same fabric. Both pieces faced a coffee table and a small television that sat upon a VCR, DVD player, and digital cable box. No TV stand. The small, Target-brand dining set to her left was covered with files and newspaper clippings, and the garbage in the kitchen overflowed with TV dinner boxes. Craig stomped into the small area and began going through his cabinets in search of food for two. From his bewildered expression as he pulled out a can of soup, Janine could tell he didn't often look in them.

A narrow hallway led to two more rooms she assumed were the bedroom and bathroom. Craig's place was more like an apartment than a house. Aside from the kitchen, it was fairly neat, but he obviously didn't spend a lot of time there. She was surprised that he had no wife waiting for him, and she correctly assumed he was divorced. She wasn't about to ask him.

Craig turned on the television, and idly waved her toward the couch. When she sat, he handed her the remote and went about making chicken noodle soup.

He kept an eye on her, experiencing an odd flutter in his gut when she swapped her sunglasses for a pair of silver, wire-rimmed eyeglasses. Suddenly his image of her went from California girl to Harvard law student, especially when he caught sight of the laptop tucked in the enormous bag she carried. He liked that image a lot better. Funny, he'd never been turned on by glasses before. He indulged in another brief fantasy in which she wore a Catholic school uniform, pigtails, and red spike heels. Mentally, he kicked himself. He hadn't gotten laid in a while. That had to be his problem.

With a start, he stirred the soup just before it boiled over, and served it in two bowls he unearthed in another mysterious cupboard.

Janine kicked off her sandals and tucked her long legs under her before taking the bowl and spoon from him. "Thanks."

Craig's blood pressure jumped again, causing his voice to roughen. "Yeah. Sorry. Table's occupied." He settled into the recliner and kicked up the foot support.

"What are the newspaper clippings about?" Janine asked conversationally.

"Nothing. Just an ongoing investigation of sorts." He dug into his soup and turned his attention to the television. Janine could easily see that this was how he spent his evenings. She was also acutely aware of the fact that he did not want her there, so she turned her attention to the screen as well.

When they finished eating, Craig set his bowl on the coffee table. Since he didn't make an effort to clean up, Janine carried their bowls into the kitchen herself. She rinsed them out, then did the same with the pot he'd used. Noticing the pile of dishes in the sink, mostly silverware and glasses, she set them on top. No way was she washing all of those. Clearing her throat, she asked if he had anything to drink.

"Yeah. There's beer in the fridge. Grab me one, too."

With a huff, Janine obliged. "Nice manners," she muttered. What a rude man. Chastising herself, she recalled that she had demanded he take her in as a houseguest. He had every right to be rude. At least he'd fed her. Determined to be pleasant, she handed him his beer, popped the top on her own, and made another attempt at conversation. "Have you lived here long?"

"Almost thirteen years. Since I got divorced." He spared her a glance.

What a surprise, Janine thought smugly. "What happened?"

"Didn't work out," his face closed up.

Just as Janine strained her brain to think of a different subject, the phone rang.

"Turner," Craig answered on the third ring.

"Turner, it's Mulroney. Just wanted to let you know that we brought Ray McMillan in for questioning."

"Get anything on him?"

"We searched the place, but he'd already cleaned it out. We have nothing to hold him on."

Craig kicked the counter. "Son of a..." He noticed Janine watching him intently, and turned his back to her. "What about assault with a deadly?"

"Can't make it stick. His employees claim he doesn't even have a gun. All we've got is a distraught daughter's accusation, and she hasn't even pressed charges."

"But I saw him," Craig complained.

"Well, you aren't high on the department's list of people to trust since you got a little rough with that last guy. Besides, you were supposed to be on suspension." Krista's voice took on a lecturing tone.

"That guy was withholding information, Krista. You know that as well as I do."

"Still. That's not the way to deal with suspects. When you finish anger management classes, the department might pay more attention."

Craig swore. "That's just bunk."

"That's the way it is. See if you can get an official statement out of the daughter. We've got to get McMillan's files."

"I'll do my best, Captain." He hung up the phone with obvious anger. For good measure, he kicked the counter again, then jumped when Janine spoke from right behind him.

"What was that about?" she asked.

"You sure are nosy, aren't you?" She simply stared him down. "Your daddy, that's what," Craig snapped. "We can't stick him on anything without your official statement. So I don't care how miserable your day's been. I need a statement, and I need it now!"

Janine stepped away from the anger in his eyes. Her chin quivered. "I don't like being bullied."

"Deal with it." Craig snagged a handheld cassette recorder off the dining table and pressed record. "This is the statement of Janine McMillan, regarding Raymond McMillan, seven thirty-four p.m., June sixteenth. Officer present, Detective Craig Turner. Speak." He held the recorder up to her as she started crying again.

"I hardly saw anything." Janine sobbed.

Schooling some patience into his voice, he encouraged her to repeat what she had seen. She took a deep breath, and started with knocking the dictionary onto the ground.

"What made you think the contents of the packet was cocaine?" Craig asked, more gently.

"Just that it was a white powder. I've seen a lot of movies and cop shows."

"So you have no real way of confirming that theory?"

"No. But when I confronted Brian Whitman, who works with my father…"

"That would be your former fiancé?" Craig interrupted.

The word 'former' cut her to the core, but she nodded. "Yes. I asked him if everything my father's ever bought for me had been paid for with drug money, and he didn't deny it."

"How long had he known that this was going on?"

"He said more than two years."

"So, you broke up with him, and then what?" Craig scribbled Brian's name on a piece of paper.

"I went to confront my father because he'd lied to me," her voice broke again. "When I reached the storeroom, I heard him speaking in Spanish to two of his employees. He said that Jose had gone to the police, and that they needed to find him and take care of him. He pointed the gun at them, and told them to kill Jose and make it look like a suicide." She cried as silently as she could over that particularly horrible memory.

"How did you know what they were saying?"

"I have a degree in Foreign Languages. I'm fluent in Spanish, French, and Mandarin Chinese."

That stopped Craig for a moment. Harvard law student, indeed. He looked impressed, and continued. "Did you know the other employees?"

"No."

"My father's employee Juan…"

"Juan, who?" Craig interrupted again.

"I don't *know*! My father saw me and told Juan to grab me. I knocked Juan down and ran out the door. My father chased me, and you picked me up. That's it."

Craig asked her a couple more questions, but she was crying too hard to answer them. He turned off the recorder, tossed a pillow and a blanket on the couch, and shut himself in his room.

Janine curled up on the uncomfortable sofa, sobbing and calling Craig all sorts of nasty names. He'd gotten what he wanted. The bastard. Although it wasn't quite eight-thirty, she drifted off to sleep, mercifully ending the worst day of her life.

As Craig lay in his comfortable bed, he thought of Ray McMillan. His instincts told him that Ray was connected somehow to the death of his own father. His ongoing investigation of that drug bust gone bad wouldn't end until his father's killer was behind bars. If he had to step all over weak people like Janine to get to the truth, then so be it.

He tossed and turned all night, riddled with guilt about the way he had treated her. He'd make it up to her somehow.

Chapter Four

Ray McMillan was panicking. It seemed as if the time had finally come for him to pay for his sins. Thank God he'd thought quickly when Janine had run away. Within an hour of her departure, he and his men had cleaned out the storage room, leaving behind them no trace of his illegal sideline.

Around six o'clock that evening, the police had come knocking on his door with a search warrant. They'd searched both his house and the bookstore, but had been unable to find anything incriminating. Then they'd brought him in for questioning.

Ray hadn't even called his lawyer when they'd brought him into interrogation. He still could not believe he'd been able to pull off the calm exterior. He probably could have won an award for his performance if he'd been an actor. On the outside, he'd played the part of an insulted, outraged pillar of the community to a tee. On the inside, he'd been quivering with fear and anguish.

He'd lost the most important thing in the world to him that afternoon. Even if the police never found anything on him, Janine knew the truth now, and she would never forgive him.

Unless he could get her to listen to him long enough for him to tell her how he'd tried to leave the drug business eighteen years ago. She was old enough to understand the terror he'd felt when he'd found that poor cat. She had to know that he'd stayed in it for her own safety. He had to try.

One thing Ray had figured out from the police was that, as of yesterday, Janine had not yet given them her statement. If she had, they'd have been able to hold him. Maybe her loyalty to her father would hold out just long enough for him to get the hell out of town.

On second thought, he had better take Brian with him as well. His daughter's fiancé had known about the drugs for a while, and he was definitely the type to give the police any information he could to save his own tail. Ray had to get to him before the cops did.

He'd also discovered through the grapevine that Janine was in the care of Detective Craig Turner. He was not the kind of man Ray wanted near his daughter.

His sources told him that Detective Turner had just come off of suspension for beating a suspect he'd been questioning about a drug bust a couple months ago. He knew that it was true because the man he'd beaten was one of Xavier's top men. There were rumors of several more similar incidents in which the detective had not been punished for his actions. Turner had a definite anger control problem. Ray could only hope that the man wouldn't take his fierce temper out on his daughter.

His hands shaking, Ray prepared to do what he knew he had to do. He had to tell Xavier what had happened. From his cell phone, he dialed the number. That old, familiar chill spread through him.

"It's the middle of the night, Raymond. Is there a problem?" The distorted voice asked in answer.

Ray's voice shook as he spoke. "She knows, Xavier." He was fifty-six years old for Pete's sake. How could a computerized voice terrify him so much?

"That's unfortunate, Raymond. How could you be so careless?"

"I'm sorry. It was out of my control." Why did he always feel as though he were a naughty child being punished by an abusive mother when he spoke to Xavier?

"Sorry isn't good enough. Has she gone to the police?"

"I don't think she's talked yet," he said quickly.

"But she's with Detective Turner, isn't she?"

Oh, Lord. How had he known that? "Yes, sir."

"You know what needs to be done, Raymond." The fragmented voice sounded evilly pleased.

"*No*," Ray was so filled with horror at the thought of killing his own daughter that his voice was barely more than a whisper.

"I suggest you take care of it before she talks. You're life depends on it."

"What are you saying?" He croaked, perspiration sliding down from his temples.

"You kill her, or I'll do it for you. Then I'll come for you."

"Xavier, I can't…" All Ray could hear was the dial tone. The low buzzing sounded like the laughter of the devil himself. "I can't kill my own daughter."

Tears of self-pity filled his once bright blue eyes as he whipped the phone at the floor. He had to do it. He had no choice. If he didn't, Xavier would. Ray couldn't even imagine the torture Janine would be forced to endure if Xavier got to her first. He couldn't let that happen.

With the simple push of a button, Ray relieved himself of the guilt that would suffocate him if he were to follow Xavier's orders. He sent two of his henchman after his own flesh and blood, and another after Brian.

Inside Ray's terror-riddled brain, something snapped.

After talking with Ray, Xavier knew that the man would never be able to kill his own daughter. He had always been weak. She was a loose end that needed to be tied. Xavier could not let a meek, frivolous man's kin cause the collapse of a powerful, successful, money making empire. It had stood strong for far too long. Thirty-six years of unquenchable greed and untold billions had poisoned Xavier's heart to any compassion for the man who loved his daughter. Childless, Xavier's solution was a simple one. The girl must die.

A simple Internet search, with a little computer hacking, produced Detective Craig Turner's address. Computers were marvelous things. Picking up the special red phone, and initiating the voice distorter, Xavier gave two faceless men their instructions.

Leaning back in a recliner as black as its owner's heart, and taking a sip of chamomile tea laced with brandy, Xavier smiled. Turner. The name struck a chord deep in the realms of memory. After a moment, revelation dawned. James Turner. That was it. He was the cop that had almost discovered Xavier's secret thirteen years ago. Xavier sneered, remembering the shock on the face of that brave man just before a bullet had pierced his heart. He'd never expected to be attacked by such a person. The element of surprise was Xavier's secret weapon. Even Xavier's own men did not know the true identity of their master. Those that did were dead. The voice distorter itself was eerie enough to command obedience, and the threat of death upon disobedience merely an incentive.

Now, thirteen years later, the son of that unfortunate cop was all but knocking on Xavier's door. It certainly was a small world after all.

At four o'clock in the morning, the rather disgruntled son in question awoke to the incessant ringing of the telephone on his nightstand. Swiping a hand over a scruff of beard, he shook himself awake and answered it.

"Turner," his voice was a sleepy croak.

"Turner, it's Mulroney. I think we found Jose. Can you bring Janine down to the station to identify him?"

"Dead?"

"Looks like a suicide." Krista told him. "As soon as possible, please. We've got to get McMillan before he skips town."

"Twenty minutes." Craig hung up the phone and pulled on a pair of jeans, not bothering to button them. Grabbing a tee shirt, he stumbled into the living room to wake sleeping beauty from her slumber on his couch. Wanting her to suffer for giving him a sleepless night, he thwacked her with his shirt.

"Ouch!" Janine cried, glaring at him. "That really wasn't necessary." She sat up, her breath catching in her throat at the sight of his well-muscled bare chest and sagging jeans as he pulled the gray shirt over his head. When his head popped through the top, she found the scruff of beard very appealing. She had rarely seen Brian like that. He'd always been clean-shaven and making breakfast by the time she'd gotten up. Groaning, she tried to rub the image from her gritty eyes. "What time is it?"

"It's four in the damn morning. Get up, princess." He started the coffeemaker, determined to at least take five minutes to wake up before heading to the station. "You have to go identify Jose for the captain."

"They found him?"

"Yeah. Dead." Like a man just come in from the burning desert, Craig gulped down the first mug of coffee. He swallowed, and waved the mug in her direction.

"Sure." Janine dug a brush out of her bag and set to work combing out the tangles in her yard of hair. To her dismay, he offered her the same mug he'd used.

"Sorry. It's the only clean one. I rinsed it out." He handed it to her, and tapped his foot until she drank it quickly. "Let's go. We've gotta catch your daddy before he leaves town."

Janine grabbed her bag, wished briefly for a shower and clean clothes, and followed him. "Do you think he will?"

"I would if I were him." He opened the passenger door of the Mustang for her, failing to notice her surprised look. When she climbed in, he slammed it shut and walked around. Starting the car, and shifting into reverse, he screeched out of the driveway.

"Do you do everything so quickly?" Janine asked, grouchy.

Craig sent her a wicked smile and winked. "Not everything, princess."

Momentarily electrified by the high voltage of his smile, Janine rolled her eyes and gazed out the window. "The sun isn't even up yet."

"Welcome to the life of a cop."

They drove the rest of the way in silence, and Janine struggled not to doze off. Unless she'd had early classes, she'd never been much of a morning person. To keep her mind busy, she tried to remember Jose as clearly as she could from their few brief meetings. When they arrived at the police station, Janine slogged up the steps as if wading through mud, while Craig practically skipped past her. She could hate him just for that.

Captain Krista Mulroney met them at the door. She shook Janine's hand with a surprisingly firm grip for such a short, round person.

"Nice to meet you," Janine said politely.

"You, too. My husband Mark is a friend of your father's."

"I guess that's too bad for him." Where had that come from? Janine really needed more coffee. To her relief, the captain laughed at her comment. "Sorry. I hate mornings."

"I'm right there with you, honey," Krista smiled. "Anyway, you seem to be holding up okay, considering everything you went through." Janine nodded. Krista patted her back, and gestured toward the lobby. "Come on inside. I'm afraid this will be unpleasant. We found him hanging from a rafter, so he doesn't look his best."

Janine braced herself. It was *really* too early in the morning to be looking at dead bodies. At least she hadn't known Jose that well. One look at his bloated face and bulging eyes had Janine feeling thankful that she hadn't had breakfast, but it was Jose. She nodded at the captain, and escaped the cold room as quickly as possible. She followed the captain and Craig into Krista's office. Craig handed over the handheld recorder he'd used the night before.

"Janine said her father told the two men to kill him and make it look like a suicide." Craig told Krista.

"Is that true?" she asked Janine. At her nod, she continued, "In that case, I guess we need to start looking more closely at suicides over the last ten years or so. Did your father ever hire anyone that wasn't of Latin American heritage?"

"Not that I can remember. Now that I look back, I realize that they were probably all illegal aliens and probably paid cash for their services. None of them ever spoke much English, except for Juan."

"We talked to him last night. He has a work Visa," Krista stated. "There were no other employees on the premises, and no record of any others except Brian Whitman, whom we have been unable to reach. How many employees would you say your father has at one time?"

"I don't really know. Not more than ten, I don't think. I guess I never paid much attention." Janine crossed her arms defensively across her chest. "I guess I should have. I really hadn't spent that much time at the bookstore before last year. I've been away at college off and on for the last nine years or so."

"Nine years of college?" Craig asked in disbelief. "What are you, a doctor?"

The corner of Janine's mouth twitched. "More like a professional student. I have degrees in Literature, Accounting, and Foreign Languages. I like learning. I had planned on running the bookstore myself someday, and thought those degrees would be helpful."

"And you never knew about your father's sideline?" Krista asked, somewhat suspiciously.

"No. Like I said, I was away a lot."

Krista decided that Janine was a trustworthy person. She was just too innocent to have been involved. "Any idea how long your father's been doing this?"

"Brian told me he's been doing it since my mother died. That was when I was two years old. I'm twenty-eight now."

"Wow." Krista wondered how on earth Ray had never gotten caught before now. "Well, we've got enough to get his files now. Craig, why don't you take Janine back to your place? She should be safe there. By the time you get back, we'll divvy up his files. You can take the paper half and work on them from home. He'll have computer files, too, right Janine?"

"Yeah. He did a lot of business on the Internet." She ran her hand through her hair, and shrugged self-consciously. "Well, I hope I helped a little."

"You did. Thanks, Janine. We'll be in touch." Krista shook her hand again, and dismissed them.

"I don't really want to be alone," Janine said to Craig as they walked out, feeling her throat tightening with tears again.

"I think you can manage an hour or two by yourself," he said, unsympathetically. "You're a big girl."

Janine didn't have the strength to argue with him. Those darn tears were sliding down her cheeks again.

Craig pretended he didn't notice she was crying again as they pulled out of the station. He didn't say a word to her until he dropped her off at his house.

"Lock the door and try to get some rest. I'll be back before you know it."

Just for good measure, he searched his property once she went inside. All clear. He didn't think her own father would come after her, but you never knew. He got back in the car and headed back into town. At least he was getting a break from her. He couldn't stand all that 'poor me' stuff. And when would she ever quit crying? Too bad such good looks were wasted on a weak woman. He couldn't stand weak women. They weren't in the dark ages anymore. Women could stand up for themselves nowadays. They didn't need knights in shining armor.

After all, his own wife had been tough enough to kick him out on the street and forbid him to ever see their son. That had been almost thirteen years ago. Ethan would almost be a teenager now. Of course, Craig had certainly never been Karen's knight in shining armor.

When Janine locked the door behind her, the tears gushed out. Oh, she was sick of crying, but she couldn't seem to stop. It was ridiculous. She probably hadn't even cried this much in her whole life before yesterday. Janine was not a crier. It had used to take some pretty strong emotions to make her break down. Now all it took was the mention of her father, or a raised voice. Pathetic.

Of course, she'd led a happy life before yesterday. Aside from her mother's death, she'd never experienced grief. Her grandparents had all died before she'd turned four, so she had never even had to experience that kind of loss. Her parents had both been only children, so she had no other relatives. So now, with the emotional loss of her father and Brian, she was utterly, and completely alone.

She curled herself up on the lumpy couch, and wept until no more tears came. Finally spent, she was determined to make herself feel better. Her first thought was a nice, hot shower. Then she remembered that she didn't have any clothes. How was she going to fix that problem? She couldn't go home.

Sighing, she tied her hair back and wandered into the kitchen. Splashing cold water on her face made her feel marginally more human. Digging into her bag, she tried to repair the damage her tears had done to her makeup.

Satisfied, she poured herself another cup of coffee, and found her gaze drawn to the newspaper clippings scattered across the dining room table. She settled onto a chair and began to pick through them. In moments she was wrapped up in the drama, and before she knew it, she'd lost two hours.

The first thing she noticed was that they were almost thirteen years old. Within minutes, she was caught up in the story of a drug bust gone bad, resulting in the death of a man who had to be Craig's father. She studied the picture of James Turner, forty-five years old when he was killed, and noticed many similarities. In a few more years, Craig would be almost identical to his father. Realizing that the person responsible for James Turner's death had never been caught, she remembered Craig's reference to 'an ongoing investigation of sorts' the day before. Suddenly feeling like she was snooping into a story Craig wouldn't want her to know about, she did her best to put the clippings back where they'd been. She'd already had a small taste of his temper.

Left alone with her thoughts, Janine's mind took an unexpected turn. Her father had mentioned someone named Xavier when he'd held the gun to his employees yesterday. What if this Xavier was her father's boss, the real brains behind the operation? Goose bumps raised on her arms. She hadn't been too worried about her father coming after her, but what if Xavier did? Her father knew that she was with the police. What if he'd passed it on to his boss? In all the movies she'd seen and stories she'd read, the leaders of drug dealing operations had been evil men with lots of power. Evil men wouldn't hesitate to kill someone who'd threatened to go to the cops.

Her father's men had already killed Jose. What if she was next? Suddenly, rather than sorrow, Janine was filled with terror. Right now she was unarmed and alone in an unfamiliar place out in the country. There could be people coming for her already.

She jumped a foot off the ground and screamed when the front door opened.

"Whoa! Give me a heart attack, why don't you!?" Craig had drawn his gun from his holster in a flash. Holding a hand out to her, he put it away.

"I'm sorry," Janine's heart was still pounding. "I was just realizing that there could be people out there planning to kill me when you got here."

"Most likely, people *are* planning to kill you. But for now, you're safe. You're with me. Nobody knows where I live. You're father's cronies don't even know who picked you up yesterday. Relax. Everything's fine." Craig was looking at her as if she'd gone crazy. With a shake of his head, he bent to pick up the package of files he'd dropped when he came in.

He heard a muffled *pop* and *whoosh* as a bullet flew through the spot in the open doorway his head had just vacated. Janine screamed as she watched it plow into the wall as if in slow motion.

"Get down!" Craig tackled her, kicked the door shut behind him, and all but threw her behind the couch.

Covering her ears with her hands, she tried to make herself disappear through the hardwood floor. She heard more pops and crashes as a stream of bullets broke through the picture window in the living room. The couch jumped as one ripped through its red plaid flesh. Janine curled herself into a ball and began to pray with all of her might.

Craig belly-crawled across the floor, gun drawn, flashing brown eyes flying from side to side. He crept to the door and kicked it open. Pressing himself flat against the wall, he peered around the corner.

A man in a ski-mask crouched and ducked along beneath the window, his head popping up to look inside.

Like the crack of a whip, Craig sprang around the doorjamb, shot the man almost point blank in the head, and flew back inside.

He listened intently over the roaring in his ears, and heard another shot fired from the back of the house. Quickly making sure the path was clear, Craig crept along the side. He heard a bullet ping off of metal, and assumed the other man had just shot the lock off of the back door.

As far as he could tell, there were only two men, and one of them was dead. Throwing caution to the wind in order to get to Janine before the second man did, he charged through the back door, firing as he went.

A bullet hit the man in front of him in the center of the back, and he fell to his knees. Craig fired a second shot directly into the back of the man's head, just to be sure.

Crisis averted for now, he quickly checked the rest of his property, confirming that there had only been two men.

He rushed back into the house, aware that more gunmen could be arriving shortly. He saw Janine cowering on the floor behind the couch, apparently unscathed, though his couch was torn to ribbons.

"Get up," he ordered her, giving her a hand. She looked scared, but there were no tears. "We can't stay here. Grab your stuff." Janine nodded, and ran for her bag.

Craig blew threw the house like a hurricane, shoving the package of files, his other gun, and his emergency stash of cash into a plastic grocery bag. He took Janine's hand, too charged to notice the spark that raced up his arm, and dragged her toward the Mustang.

Grateful that his baby had survived the battle without so much as a slashed tire, he hustled Janine into it, and tore out of the driveway, heading north.

He flipped his phone open and called the captain to let her know what had happened and that he and Janine would be on the run for awhile. Assured that he would be reimbursed for his expenditures, he settled back in the seat, content to drive at least two hours away from the city.

"You okay?" he asked Janine, with real concern in his eyes. When she nodded, still with no trace of tears, he felt instantly better. "We're going to be jumping around for awhile. Are you going to need anything?"

"Clothes," Janine said in a shaking voice. "And a really, really hot shower."

"Me too," Craig said with a laugh. "We'll stop in the next big city."

Chapter Five

"Thank you," Janine spoke a short while later. "I don't even want to think about what might have happened if you hadn't come home when you did."

"Just doing my job," Craig stated.

For reasons she couldn't place, Janine felt insulted by his comment. "Well, I appreciate it anyway. Where are we going?"

"No place in particular. I'm just going to drive until we find somewhere to get you those clothes, then we'll be looking for a motel. I'd feel safer if we were at least a couple hours away from the city."

"All right." Janine settled in for a long drive. Her hands were still shaking. Everything had happened so fast that she'd barely had time to react. She couldn't believe that her own father was trying to kill her. Of course, in his twisted mind, she was probably just a small step above the men he hired to do his dirty work, and he obviously had no problem ordering them to be killed. To her relief, she felt more anger about her situation now than sadness. She was just thankful that she wasn't crying. Craig was probably thankful, too.

What must he think of her? She thought about the short time they'd known each other, and how many times she'd cried when she was with him. It was really very embarrassing. He probably thought that she was the epitome of the 'helpless, blubbering female' he'd previously referred to her as. Even though it really didn't matter what Craig thought about her, Janine was determined to do some damage control. She had an unfounded desire for him to know who she really was. It was probably because he was the only one that hadn't known the real her before all this madness, and she was different now.

"Why did you decide to become a cop?" Janine angled her body to face him.

A little surprised at the question, Craig glanced at her. "Why?"

Janine rolled her eyes. "It's called conversation, Craig. Since we're going to be spending a lot of time together in the near future, it wouldn't hurt for us to get to know one another."

Craig enjoyed the way his name sounded in that husky voice, dripping with frustration. That had been the first time she'd used it. "My father was a cop. There wasn't ever anything else I wanted to do."

"Do you like it?"

"It has its good moments and bad moments. This morning was a bad moment."

"I'll say," Janine agreed. She knew he'd killed the two men that had come after her because he'd had no choice. "Do you ever feel guilty when you have to kill people like you did today?"

"Not when they're the bad guys. I've kind of grown immune to that over the years. I sure as hell don't *like* to do it, but most of the time, it's you or them. So far, I've always made sure it was them." He sent her a small smile. "What do you do?"

"Me?"

"No, the other person in the car with me."

What did she do? "Well, I'm kind of a professional student, like I told your captain. I've never worked anywhere besides the bookstore."

"And you liked living like that?" Craig couldn't understand not having some sort of purpose in your life. "I mean, before the last two days."

"Yes. I was really close to my father before all this happened. He was my best friend." Janine cursed her voice as it cracked again. Determined not to cry anymore, she cleared her throat. "It was great getting to spend all that time with him. And Brian. I liked dealing with the customers, and being surrounded by all those books. There's nothing

I like doing more than immersing myself in a good book. I guess I always knew my father would pass the bookstore over to me someday, just like his father did for him and his grandfather had done for his father."

"You really spend all your free time reading? Don't you have any friends?" Craig had probably read two books in his entire life once he'd finished college, and he had no idea why someone would want to spend so much time doing something so boring.

Janine huffed. "My father and Brian were my whole world. I liked it that way. So what if I don't have any other friends. All you really need is a couple of people to talk to, and I had that. I didn't see hordes of friends knocking on your door, either," she told him pointedly.

"I'm a cop. I don't have friends."

They rode in silence for a while.

When Janine could no longer stand it, she decided to brave Craig's temper and asked him the question that had been circling in her mind since that morning. "What happened to your father?"

Craig looked at her quickly. "How do you know about that?"

Janine felt a blush creeping into her cheeks. "I might have glanced at those newspaper clippings while you were gone."

"You sure are nosy." He bit down on his temper. After a few more minutes, he decided he could share that part of his history with her. If her father was connected, maybe she'd know something that could help him in his ongoing investigation. "My father was a narcotics cop. He loved his job. Just like me, there was never anything else that appealed to him. He was a good cop. His partner wasn't."

He took his time putting his words together. The thought of what his father's partner had done still made him angry after all these years. "My father had stumbled upon a major drug ring in the course of his investigations. No one knows the details of it. His files were destroyed by his partner before anyone figured out what had happened. I was twenty-one at the time, new to the force, and not important enough to know all that went on. All I know is that my father had an informant that he trusted more than he should have. The informant worked for him for more than six months, feeding him tidbits here and there to steer him on the right course. He went undercover at the end and set up a meeting with the person he was sure was in charge of the business, under the guise of being interested in joining the dealers. He and his partner, Mick Reilly," Craig's teeth clenched at the name, "had an appointment to meet the boss at a warehouse my dad was pretending to work at. I remember him dressing up in a grungy uniform before he left that day, telling me to wish him luck and that he'd see me in the morning. I didn't even get the chance to tell him I loved him and how proud I was of him."

Janine looked at him with sympathy swimming in her brown eyes. She could picture him, young and naïve, much as she had been until recently. When Craig was quiet for a while, she urged him to continue. "What happened?"

"The plan was for them to go in and make the deal with the boss, and that back up would show up exactly fifteen minutes later. The parking lot was quiet when they arrived. I think they were early. They got out of the vehicle and crept up. Apparently, they walked in on a murder. The boss was unhappy with a couple of the underlings, and had chosen that night to make them pay. The worst part of it was that the informant *was* the boss. The informant had been feeding my father bogus information to keep him running in circles, but I think Dad had figured that out. My father must have known he'd been set up as soon as he'd recognized his informant. He told his partner to call for back up, that the plan had to be aborted. Of course, his partner conveniently forgot to do as he asked."

"Mick confessed later that he even lead my father to the boss at gunpoint. My father was killed face to face by the informant he'd trusted, and we found out later that Mick helped the informant escape by waiting until after my dad had been shot to call in the back up. He even had the informant shoot him so it would look like he'd had to fight for his life. Turned out Mick Reilly was a dealer himself. I figured that much out, and I made sure he went to prison for what he'd done to my father. It took me over six months to find enough proof that he was involved, but he got what he deserved. He never would tell us who the informant was or any details of my dad's investigation.

Apparently, he's decided he'd rather spend his entire worthless life in prison than rat out his supplier. I'm going to figure out who that informant was if it's the last thing I do. I'm going to break down that drug ring bit by bit, and then I'm going to kill the man in charge."

"I'm so sorry," Janine said quietly. The anger and deep-rooted bitterness in his voice made her heart clutch for the young man who'd lost his father so unfairly.

Her curiosity satisfied, she left Craig to his thoughts until they arrived at a department store. Thankful that she had room on her credit card, Janine bought a few days worth of clothes and toiletries that would tide her over until she was finally able to return home. Whenever she found a home.

An hour later, they found a shabby motel a little ways off the highway. Craig checked them in, and unlocked the door to the room, carrying both their bags inside. It was one of those motels where the rooms look like a garden exploded on the walls and carpet. It was tacky, but it would do for now.

Janine headed straight for the bathroom and, locking the door behind her, indulged herself in that really, really hot shower. When she'd finished, she felt slightly better. She dried her hair with the wall mounted dryer, and pulled on the green and blue plaid boxer shorts and oversized dark blue tee shirt she'd bought. Slipping her feet into a pair of extremely fluffy slippers, she prepared to offer her help to Craig in his investigation.

The second she walked out of the room, Craig walked in, trying his best not to admire the long length of tan leg peeking out from those little shorts. Janine pulled Nora Roberts' *Birthright* out of her book bag, stretched out on the single full-sized bed, and entertained herself for the half hour he was in the bathroom. She'd never known a man to take so long.

When Craig finally emerged, a cloud of steam following him out the door, Janine sat up and pulled her laptop out. "I want to help with the investigation."

"What for?" Craig asked.

"I want to know exactly what my father's been up to all these years. Besides, I thought you might like to use my laptop. It's got wireless Internet."

"Sure. Can't hurt." He went to his own bag and pulled the package of files out, handing them to her. "You can help me go through these. Look for repeat customers over the last several years. We know he sends the drugs to his customers in books. We need to figure out which books those might be so we can take down his clientele as well if at all possible."

"The book I knocked over was Webster's Dictionary."

"Good. So look for dictionaries first. The problem is, even if there are certain books, other people that aren't involved may order those books, too. He's got to have some kind of system of codes or something. We don't really have much so far. Seems like your father's sideline is very complicated and well thought out."

"That's how he got away with it for so long. The thing is, Craig, I just can't picture my father coming up with this on his own. He's smart, but he's not diabolical. There has to be somebody else behind it." In all that had happened that morning, Janine had forgotten the name Xavier.

"Then we need to look into his suppliers. If he isn't the top man, one of his suppliers is. It's likely that the one behind it has a bookstore as a front as well. So, you look for books, and I'll make a list of all of his suppliers." He glanced around the room, shook his head. "Or I would make a list if I had some paper."

Janine pulled a notebook and a couple of pens out of her book bag.

Craig raised an eyebrow. "I thought you said you were done with school?"

"I am. It never hurts to have a spare notebook around." Janine tore a sheet of paper out of the notebook and passed it to Craig. Settling back against the headboard of the bed, pushing her glasses up on her nose, she opened the first file. Craig skimmed through his files for about ten minutes, then set them aside to find a rock station on the little bedside alarm clock. As he bent over the little dial, the scent of the soap Janine had used assailed his nostrils. He glanced up, and felt his heart bump at how close she was. She sat cross-legged on the bed, her little shorts riding dangerously high on her thighs. Her head was bent, and her hair rained over her shoulders, revealing the nape of her very slender neck. Thankful that she wasn't looking at him, he clamped down on a sudden urge to bite just there, and stood up, clearing his throat. What was wrong with him?

"Sorry. I hate quiet." Craig resumed his place at the little desk by the window, deliberately turning his back on her.

The day wore on until Craig tossed his pile aside. "Okay, I've got a list of the suppliers in this bunch."

Janine shifted her focus from her pile to him. She glanced at her piece of paper, on which she'd written Webster's Dictionary followed by twenty-five stick numbers. "Well, I've got twenty-five dictionary orders, but that really isn't very many in the ten years these files cover. I can't figure out what the other books might be. There's a lot of Dean Koontz, Stephen King, Danielle Steele, Nora Roberts, Dan Brown, Nicholas Sparks, and a bunch of other well-known writers."

"That might be a dead end. I mean, he could easily have stashed drugs in any number of those books, any bestsellers, pretty much anything he wanted. Obviously they never made any mistakes with their shipments or we'd have heard about it. It'd be a little bit of a shock if you were midway through your favorite author's new best seller and a packet of cocaine fell in your lap. I wish there was a way we could figure out the codes. But without actually talking to people who used the system, there's no way we'd know, and since we can't determine who was receiving drugs, I don't even know who we'd start with." He stood up and paced the small room, thinking out loud. "How would they order? Wouldn't cocaine cost more than even a huge shipment of books? He must have had a way to charge them for the book order, then some separate system of wire transfers or something. But his income hasn't increased more than it should at least in the last couple of years." He stopped at the window, gazed out at the empty parking lot.

"What about Swiss numbered accounts? They always have numbered accounts in books and movies." Janine suggested, shifting to sit at the end of the bed.

Craig nodded. "That could work. Did you ever see your dad with a large amount of cash? He could have stashed it somewhere in the house."

"He always had cash, but I don't remember it being large amounts. A couple hundred at most. There really wasn't anywhere he could have stashed it in our house, except for a small wall safe in his office."

"Yeah. A wall safe wouldn't hold the amounts of cash I'd think he'd have. Then again, maybe he doesn't have a huge clientele. He could get rich off ten regulars at the price cocaine goes for."

"There weren't any customers that stood out more than others as regulars in my pile, at least that I noticed."

"Mine either. As often as an addict needs cocaine, they must have had a few different names to go by, or bought the product from more than just your dad's bookstore. We're dealing with shipping drugs through the mail. They could be ordering from Japan, for God's sake. Let's just focus on the suppliers. You look at my list here and see if you're familiar with any of these, and I'll take your pile."

Janine traded with him and skimmed over his list with her brow furrowed. "Most of these are wholesalers. If any of his suppliers are involved in this, I don't think it would be a wholesaler. It would have to be an independent distributor, and he has several of those as well."

"What about rare books? Would he stash drugs in those?" Craig asked. Janine looked at him with such horror at the thought that he had to laugh. "Guess not."

"Whatever else he may be, my father is a book collector. He would *never* mar a rare book. He'd cut off his own hand first."

"Okay. Forget I said that. Do you know which ones are independent distributors?"

"Yes. They're usually other bookstores that he shares inventory with. Sister stores of sorts. You have a few of them on your list: Bailey's Books in Forest Lake, Johnson's in St. Paul, Rare Books and More and Low Price Adventures out of Minneapolis."

"We'll start by checking out each one of those stores and see if we notice anything suspicious. We should probably wait a day or two to head back down to the city since those two men were probably not the only ones after you." He ran a hand through his shaggy hair, and glanced at his watch. One o'clock and they hadn't eaten anything all day. "How about we grab a late lunch somewhere, then come back and see what we can find on the Internet."

Janine's stomach rumbled at the mention of food. "Sounds good to me."

"You like pizza? I saw a Pizza Hut a few miles back."

"Who doesn't?" Janine stood up and realized how she was dressed. She wasn't going anywhere in her lounging shorts. "Let me change first."

Craig rolled his eyes, and tapped his foot while she dragged her bag into the bathroom. "Women." He muttered. She emerged a short while later looking scrumptious in pale jean shorts and a pink midriff tank top. He felt water pool in his mouth. The shirt was pink for heaven's sake. Was he really that desperate? "Ready?"

Janine nodded, swapping her glasses for sunglasses once again, and they headed out, locking the door behind them.

They settled into a booth at the Pizza Hut and Janine persuaded Craig to order Stuffed Crust Pizza, her all time favorite, but let him choose the toppings.

"So tell me about your ex-wife," Janine said, taking a bite of gooey garbage pizza.

"Why?" Craig asked, digging in to his own.

"Once again, it's called conversation, Craig."

"Once again, you sure are nosy. What do you want to know?"

"Why did you get divorced?" Janine sipped her Pepsi.

"What makes you think knowing me for one day gives you the right to know everything about me?" Craig glared at her over his slice of pizza.

"Well, I don't have much choice than to tell you everything about me, seeing as how you are investigating my father. It only seems fair."

"Fine. Her name is Karen. We were only married for a year. It didn't work out," he said gruffly.

Janine blinked at him for a moment. "Wow. That's just bursting with details."

SHATTERED ILLUSIONS

Craig rolled his eyes, resigned to tell her the whole story. He'd never see her again after the investigation was over, so what difference did it make? "When my father was killed, I went a little crazy. I was so angry and confused that I couldn't even see straight. I was obsessed with finding out who'd done that to him, and I let everything else slide. She didn't like that much. She really didn't like that when she tried to talk to me about it, I went berserk. I trashed our living room, and she kicked me out and told me never to come back. She was about six months pregnant at the time, and she's never even let me see our son, Ethan. You happy now?"

"Sorry." Janine said meekly. She really was nosy. "I didn't think it would be that kind of a story."

"Not all of us have had the easy life you've had. I've had a little bit of a temper problem since my father was killed, so try not to push me too far."

"I consider myself warned." Janine shut her mouth and finished her meal.

When they returned to the motel, they switched on Janine's laptop and researched all the bookstores on the Internet. Nothing stood out, and by nine o'clock that evening, they called it a day. Janine curled up on the bed while Craig slept on the floor with his gun.

Craig spent another sleepless night feeling bad about the way he'd treated Janine. He really did have a temper problem. That was probably something he should work on. Tomorrow he would do his best to be nice to her all day. She'd had a rough time lately.

Chapter Six

Janine awoke the next morning to the sounds of Madonna coming from the vicinity of her book bag. Groggily remembering her cell phone, she dove for it. Seeing her father's cell phone number in the caller identification, she paled and glanced at Craig.

"Does that thing have a speakerphone?" he asked her. She nodded. "Turn it on and pay close attention to everything he says. Damn, I wish there was a way I could track it from here."

She did as he asked. "Hello?" she asked timidly.

"Neeny! Thank God," came Ray's voice, loud and clear. "Where are you? Are you okay?"

She felt her heart hardening, and those darn tears threatening again. "What makes you think I even want to talk to you?"

"I know you're upset, Neeny..." Ray began.

"Upset?" Janine's voice was dangerously low. "Why would I be upset about finding out that you've lied to me for my entire life? How long, Dad? How long?"

"Please let me explain," Tears thickened his voice. "I didn't have a choice. Your mom died and I was left with mountains of debt. I would have had to sell the bookstore. You know that would have broken you're grandfather's heart if he'd been alive. I was about to do it when I got the letter, but I just couldn't. It sounded like a simple solution. He promised me it would only be for a short while."

"Do you think that makes it okay?"

"No, Neeny! I tried to leave it after we went on that camping trip...you remember don't you? We had so much fun that weekend."

Janine choked back tears at the memory that burst through her mind of her dad teaching her to fish. It had been one of the best weekends of her whole life. "Why didn't you?"

"He threatened to kill you if I did! He left a dead cat on our doorstep! I couldn't take that kind of risk. You're everything to me! I had no choice! I had no choice, Neeny."

"You could have turned him over to the police."

"I couldn't. He'd have killed you anyway, and I'd have ended up in prison. There was no other way! He's crazy! He's after you now, I know he is. Are you okay?"

"I've already survived one gun battle, no thanks to you."

He gasped. "Thank God you're all right. What about the cop? Turner? Has he hurt you?"

"Why would he hurt me, Dad? He saved my life yesterday."

"He has a terrible temper, Janine. He's beaten suspects in all sorts of cases. He's a bad cop. He's dangerous! Tell me you'll be careful!"

Janine glanced at Craig with a trace of fear; he shook his head at her. Little temper problem? "I can trust him better than I can trust you now. He's all I have left. You're nothing to me."

Ray broke down into heart-wrenching sobs. "Don't say that, baby. Please don't say that. You have to forgive me! I can give you a great life. I have millions hidden away. You'll never have to worry about anything again! Please forgive me. I'm your father!"

"You're nothing." She repeated, breaking down into sobs of her own. "You think I want your drug money? Forget it. I can make my own money. It's pathetic that that's all you have left to offer me. Not your love, just your drug money."

Craig broke in. "Tell us who your boss is, Ray, and you may not spend your entire sorry life in prison. Give her that much."

"Don't even talk to me, Turner. You hurt her, I'll hunt you down and break your neck," Ray shouted, anger breaking through the sobs.

"You've hurt her enough for the both of us, McMillan."

"Neeny, I've got Brian here. He wants to talk to you. Listen to him, he's a good man. He was never involved. He just kept my secret. Please don't throw your life away!"

Janine felt fear clutch in her chest. What was Brian doing with him? Had he lied, was her father lying now, about never being involved?

"Janine!" Brian called. "Please forgive us. We love you so much. I can't live without you, baby. You've got to reconsider. We can forget this whole thing. I can take care of you!"

"Brian, I said the wedding is off. Try to get that through your thick head. You're as bad as he is. I can't trust you. If I can't trust you, I can't be with you. I told you that already! Why are you with him? Are you helping him?"

"No, Janine! We're worried about you. Where are you? Xavier's after you!"

Janine jerked at the name. How had she forgotten that? She saw Craig jot the name down, with a question mark, and tried to gain control of her tears. "He's already found me once. I'm not telling you where we are. How do I know you aren't passing on the information? I can't trust either of you!"

"Please, Janine. I need you! Forgive me!" Brian was sobbing now, begging and pleading with her to understand and to come back to him.

"I never want to see you again!" Janine shouted back on a sob. "Leave me alone!"

Brian began crying so hard that Janine could no longer understand a word he said. Her father's voice came back on the line.

"Neeny, he wants me to kill you. I can't do that, you know that, don't you? I could never.... You're everything to me!"

"I don't care, *Ray*." She couldn't even bring herself to call this man her father anymore. "It wouldn't surprise me if you did kill me. Everything you ever told me was a lie. *Everything*! I don't even know if you ever really loved me. I never want to see you again, Ray. Never!"

Ray flinched at the fact that she wouldn't even call him 'Dad.'

His heart broke. He knew he'd lost her. His already shattered mind broke even further. He had to make her see! He pulled a gun out of the waistband of his pants. "Janine, listen to me. Don't go to the police. Please don't help them anymore than you already have. I don't want to go to prison!"

Craig jumped in again. "That's where you're heading, Ray. I'm going to make sure of it. That's what you deserve! We'll find Xavier, too, and we'll bring him down as well. You're finished, McMillan. Deal with it."

Ray howled into the phone. Suddenly, Janine and Craig could hear Brian shouting in the background. He sounded scared to death. Janine couldn't breathe.

"Dad!" She shouted. "What are you doing? Leave him alone! You're in enough trouble as it is! Dad!"

"I'm finished, Neeny! There's nothing left for me. This is your last chance. Will you forgive me?" Ray shouted, his voice rising.

Brian's shouts filled her ears, shrieking that he had a gun, and she steeled her heart against them. The father she knew wouldn't shoot him, would he? She dared to call his bluff. "I can't, Dad. I'm going to help make sure you go to prison. Craig's right. It's what you deserve for everything you've put me through."

"You leave me no choice, Janine. I have to make you see. I don't want to do this." She could almost see him taking aim at Brian.

"No! Help me! Janine! Help me! I love you!" Brian howled.

Janine panicked. What had she done? She couldn't believe what was happening. She hadn't believed he'd really do it. Her father, her best friend, wasn't capable of that kind of evil. Was he? Desperate, she grabbed the phone, held it up with a grip like iron and shouted, "Daddy! *No!* I forgive you! *I forgive you!*"

Suddenly, they heard a gunshot and Brian fell silent. Oh, God. What had he done?

"It's too late now, Neeny. It's too late for all of us." With that, Ray was gone.

Janine dropped the phone as if it had started on fire and screamed, scrambling across the bed. "Oh, my God! Oh, my God! What just happened?" She turned grief stricken eyes to Craig. "*What happened?* He killed Brian! Oh, my God! Brian!" She burst into sobs, heart breaking, and curled up on the bed, weeping.

Craig's hands were shaking. He hadn't thought Ray was capable of it either, or he would have stopped her from calling his bluff. His heart went out to Janine as she curled herself into a ball, weeping as if her life was over. He suddenly had a suspicion that it was. Clumsily, he sat on the bed and pulled her to him, feeling her tears seep through the tee shirt he wore. He patted her back, stroked her hair and held her tight, trying to stop her from shaking so badly. He felt helpless. He shushed her, pressed his lips to her head.

And suddenly found his mouth on hers.

She quieted and clung to him, assaulting his lips with her own. The taste of him was all man. Strength, protection, confidence...everything she needed right now. Mostly she needed love. She wanted him to make love to her, to clear her mind of all these hurts. She pulled him down on top of her, hands racing up under his shirt, frantic to feel flesh on flesh.

"Make love to me," she moaned softly, pressing him to her. "Make me forget."

Craig felt heat rush into him. God, he wanted her. He didn't know any other way to comfort her. His hands slid beneath her tank top, clutching at the small, perky breasts. Her scent assailed him, her warmth seeped into him. A wild need filled him to possess. He reached down to undo the button on her shorts.

And snapped back to his senses. What was he doing? She was distraught! He couldn't take advantage of her like that! What kind of an animal was he? He jumped off of her as if he'd been burned and paced to the window, wiping a hand across his face. He tried to regain his control. Without even glancing at her, he went into the bathroom and locked the door. Stripping off his clothes, and turning the water on as cold as possible, he stepped in and regained his sanity with a yelp.

Janine watched him go, flustered, confused, heart pounding. The charges his kiss had sent through her were still tingling. She'd never felt anything like it before. What had she done? Throwing herself at the only man that was available just because she needed to forget what had happened? That wasn't who she was! Janine McMillan was a strong, independent, brave woman. Or at least she'd used to be. Tears began anew, and she buried her face in her pillow. Numb with shock, she drifted into sweet, comforting oblivion.

When Janine awoke it was evening and everything had changed. She felt hollowed out, nothing but an empty shell where a strong woman had once been. Her thoughts flew to her father, and to her relief, no tears came. Instead, she felt hatred. She was filled with loathing and disgust toward the man who had raised her. The man who was no longer her father.

He'd killed the man she'd loved. For that, he would never be forgiven.

Despite the fact that she had called off the wedding, Brian had still held a place in her heart. Now that place was locked tight, never to be opened again. She could no longer afford to love.

The old Janine was gone. She had been a woman who had believed that life was wonderful, that evil would never touch her. In her place was a woman filled with a need for vengeance. Ray would pay for what he had done.

Now all she had to do was survive long enough to make sure he did.

Burying the helpless, blubbering female she had become over the last few days, Janine pulled herself up and glanced around for Craig. She saw him at the desk, using her laptop to search the Internet with his shaggy hair falling over his eyes.

Suddenly reminded of that searing kiss, she felt a pull low in her belly. Then she recalled the rejection that had followed it, and her voice went frosty.

"Teach me how to shoot a gun," Janine demanded.

Craig jumped, unaware that she had woken up. He glanced at her, momentarily startled to see that her eyes were burning not with tears, but with anger. She looked good mad. Unfortunately, he now knew she tasted good as well. "How are you feeling?"

"I'm fine, no thanks to you," she snapped, running a hand through her hair and glaring at him. "I'm going to learn to protect myself, and you're going to teach me. As soon as possible."

Craig bit down on his angry retort. "I don't like being bossed around, but since I happen to agree with you, I'll obey this time. Don't try it again. It's too late to do it tonight since the light's going. First thing tomorrow morning I'll turn you into a sharpshooter. That's a promise."

Janine nodded once and marched into the bathroom to wash off the day's events.

When she returned, Craig wasn't there. Momentarily afraid, she glanced out the window. Reminding herself bitterly that he was unlikely to abandon such an important witness, she turned to the laptop he'd left on the desk. The familiar McMillan Booksellers website gave her a pang. What was going to happen to the business? Her great-grandfather's pride and joy would be ruined. Whatever happened, she'd try her best to make sure that didn't occur. Once Ray was in prison, she'd take over. After the smear on their reputation this whole thing would undoubtedly leave, it would take a while for business to get back to normal, but she knew it would. She'd make sure it did.

She pushed her glasses up, and stared at the screen. How would the customers be able to get what they were after? Did they come in personally or do it over the Internet? It had to be the Internet since they wouldn't want anyone to be able to identify them. So how did they do it?

She focused on the square on the checkout screen that read 'promotional codes or coupons.' That had to be it. Once they figured out the codes, it would be relatively easy to determine which customers were after drugs and which ones were legitimate. She wished Craig had been assigned to the computer files instead of the paper files.

Her thoughts drifted to Brian. The man of her dreams with so much left to do in his life was gone. Killed by her very own father. She wiped away the single tear that fell onto her cheek. Probably the only tear she had left. Whatever Brian had been, he hadn't deserved that. She'd make Ray pay for ending his life so crassly. So heartlessly. For no reason except to show his daughter what he was capable of.

He'd gone off the deep end. What demented part of his brain thought that she would come crawling back to him if he threatened to hurt Brian?

Resigned that there could no longer be even a trace left of the father she'd once cherished, Janine sighed. At least she'd be able to put him away for it. The sad thing was that she no longer even cared what happened to her father. He'd done that.

She knew that if necessary, she'd kill him without hesitation. The man who'd raised her. The man who'd ruined her.

Janine glanced up as the door to the motel room opened, feeling her heart stop.

Craig strode in, looking like an angry tiger, water dripping from his hair. She hadn't even noticed that it was raining.

He glared at her, and tossed her one of the grease-spotted bags he carried. "Hope you like cheeseburgers."

Janine's stomach growled as if on command. She opened the bag and dug in. Craig flopped on the bed with his own burger, and picked up the paper files that were now strewn about.

He thought of what he'd almost done on this very bed, and felt guilt stab him again. He glanced at her, sitting there at the desk in leggings and a tee shirt, perfect hair shiny and smooth again, unreasonably sexy glasses perched on her nose, and hated himself for regretting the fact that it hadn't happened. He polished off his cheeseburger, and ran a hand through his hair, scattering raindrops on the bedspread. Clearing his throat, he dared to bring it up. "Look, about before…."

"I don't know what you're talking about." Janine cut him off, ice coating her voice.

"Oh, give me a break. You were crying!" His voice rose to a shout. "I wasn't going to take advantage of you like that. I'm not that desperate." Whoops. Wrong thing to say.

Janine flew up from the chair, glaring at him, brown eyes practically shooting off sparks. "Do I look desperate to you? Do you think I'd have had any trouble getting you into the sack if I'd really wanted to?" Desperately, she tried to forget the fact that she'd practically begged him. "I could have you begging on your knees in a second."

"Hold on a minute…." Craig held his hands up as if to ward off a blow, feeling anger course through him. "I don't beg. I don't have to beg."

"Oh, believe me, I could make you." Janine crossed her arms across her chest, tilted her chin up, looking very queen of the manor.

"Whatever, Janine. I'm sorry I even brought it up. Forget it." Craig shook his head and dug into his French fries.

"Believe me, that won't be hard to do. It wasn't that memorable." She sat down on the desk chair again with enough force to break it, had she been heavier.

"Low blow, Janine. Low blow." Deliberately, Craig turned his back on her and focused on the files again.

Janine felt guilt poking her. He was right. That had been a low blow, and very untrue. If she let herself, she could still feel his lips on hers. What was she doing thinking that way about another man, when her fiancé had just been killed, anyway? What kind of woman did that make her? Despite what she'd implied to Craig, her love life was very bland. Brian had been the only man she'd ever been with, the only one she'd ever loved, and he was gone.

Now she was stuck with Craig, and despite her attempts to deny it, she was attracted to him. Why else would her heart stop when he strode into the room? Why couldn't she get that image of his very fine bare chest out of her mind? Why else had she flung herself at him the way she had? She wasn't like that. She'd been with Brian for a year and a half before she'd thrown herself at him.

She smiled at the memory that brought on, and was glad she was able to. She'd get revenge for Brian, if it were the last thing she did. Hopefully she hadn't destroyed the fledgling relationship she had going with Craig and he would help her do it.

They passed the rest of the evening in silence, each carefully pretending that the other didn't exist until Craig finally dozed off on the bed. Janine rolled her eyes at his lack of courtesy and read her book in the lone recliner until the wee hours of the morning when she was finally able to end another terrible day.

Chapter Seven

Craig awoke with a raging headache the next morning. He sat up, holding a hand to his head, and noticed that he was lying on the bed. He saw Janine curled up in the recliner across the room, and felt a little guilty at his lack of consideration. His mother had taught him better than that. Downing a couple of ibuprofen, he jumped in the shower, careful not to wake her. When she was still sleeping when he walked out of the bathroom, he gave her the same rude awakening he'd given her at his house. He smacked her with his shirt.

"Ouch!" She cried. "What's *wrong* with you?" She sat up and glared at him, ignoring the delectable sight of his bare chest to the best of her ability. "You could just shake me for a change or something!"

"Come on, sleeping beauty. You get to learn how to defend yourself today. The earlier we get going the better. I have a feeling you're a slow learner." With a wry smile, he marched over to the two cup coffee maker and started a pot.

Janine gave a frustrated groan, and headed into the bathroom. She drank a quick Styrofoam glass of coffee when she emerged, and was hurriedly shuffled out the door. "Do you even know where we're going?" she asked him when she'd climbed into the car.

"Yeah. Ever heard of the yellow pages?" He sent her a wink. He was in a good mood now that his headache had gone away. "There's a gun range twenty minutes from here, and a place where I can pick up some more ammunition."

"Well aren't you just Mr. Prepared." Janine was not in such a good mood. She was still raw about having slept on a very uncomfortable recliner. The four hours of sleep she'd gotten probably hadn't helped either.

"Have you ever shot a gun before?" Craig asked her, ignoring her snippiness.

"No. But I know karate."

"Good for you. Doesn't work well when the bad guys are far away, though." Craig laughed when Janine stuck her tongue out at him. "Cheerful this morning, aren't we?"

"Why don't you try sleeping in a recliner."

His smile vanished. "Yeah. Sorry about that. I'd have let you have the bed if I had been awake long enough."

"Whatever. Let's just get two beds next time we get to stay at a motel."

"Agreed." He smiled again, and pulled one of his guns out of its holster, passing it to her. "Anyway. This is a Beretta 9mm Model 92FS compact pistol. It's not necessarily standard police issue, but I like it."

"Whatever that means," Janine mumbled. The gun felt cool in her hand, made her feel powerful. "It's light."

"That's because it's compact."

"Funny. How many shots?"

"I use an eight shot magazine."

"Ever killed anybody with this?" Janine looked at him curiously.

"You mean besides the two guys that attacked us at my house? Yes."

"How many?"

"It's not nice to keep count. But probably about five or six. I've injured a whole lot more than that with it. It's a last resort to shoot the bad guy if you can avoid it. I find it much more satisfying to watch them rot in prison if their lawyers don't help them wriggle out of it."

"I can understand that. That's where my father's going if I can help it."

"We'll get him there, don't worry."

Janine was relieved that she hadn't completely destroyed their relationship the night before. He was kind of fun when he was in a good mood, something that seemed to happen very rarely.

Three hours later, Janine's nerves were shot. Her ears were ringing despite the ear plugs she'd worn, her arms were sore from holding even that light gun up that long, and her skin was tingling from having him pressed so close to her for that extended a time period. She didn't think she'd ever be able to get the seductive scent of his cologne out of her nose, but she'd finally managed to hit the target on seven out of eight shots, nicking it with the last one. They weren't necessarily fatal wounds, but they'd definitely stop someone.

"Okay. I can't do anymore today." She handed Craig back his gun and let her arms down. They felt as if they weighed fifty pounds each.

"You did surprisingly well. Maybe you aren't such a slow learner." Craig spoke to her over her shoulder, his mouth dangerously close, his hands on her hips.

"Gee, thanks, you're so sweet." Despite her best intentions, she felt her gaze drawn to his lips. She could feel her own tingle with anticipation. That had to stop. "Now back off." She shoved him back, relieved when there was finally some distance between them. She couldn't take much more of him being so close.

"Okay, okay." Deliberately, he clamped down on his own desire. How did she manage to make him feel like that? Had to be that lack of intimacy he'd been suffering from lately. "I'll get you a spare holster at some point so you can carry the gun around with you, in case we ever get separated. For now, let's get back to the motel and see what we can dig up about this Xavier."

"Sounds good."

"So what level did you make it to in Karate?"

"Black belt, of course. I always achieve my goals." She smiled at him.

"That's good. You could probably whoop me at hand to hand combat, then. I prefer fists." She had a beautiful smile. Was that the first time he'd seen it? Before he could stop himself, he touched his lips to hers.

She jerked as if she'd been burned at the contact. "Stop that." The smile vanished.

Craig felt himself flush, embarrassed he'd let himself slip like that. "Sorry." He took two very long strides to create more distance between them. Silently, he cursed himself. She was getting to him.

Janine laid a hand on her stomach when he walked ahead of her. It was quivering. It was ridiculous, this attraction between them. It was almost volatile. Had she ever felt that way with Brian? Not that she could recall. She'd never gotten stirred up merely through that brief of a kiss with him. It was something to think about- or something not to.

They drove back to the motel in silence, each one battling with their thoughts of the other. Janine followed him onto the porch, and ran right into him when he opened the door and stopped short.

"Son of a..." he swore. He pushed Janine aside and pulled out his gun, going into a crouch. "Stay here."

"What's wrong?" Janine asked, heart pounding.

"Someone's been in here. They may still be here. Stay put."

Janine peered around the doorjamb, and gasped. Someone had trashed their room. What few clothes they had were strewn about, ripped into little more than confetti. Her precious laptop had been smashed, the paper files had been torn up, and the bed and recliner had been slashed. Her bag lay upside down on top of the pile of its contents. "What were they looking for?"

"I have no idea. They ripped the files. That's the only thing I can think of. They're gone now. Long gone, I'm sure. I'm going to look around." He strode out the door.

Janine dashed into the room and dug into the pile of her belongings. Her wallet, money and credit cards included, was still there. What kind of people break into a room and don't take anything? Besides the clothes, the rest of her things were intact. She stomped over to her laptop and swore viciously, glad no one was around to hear it. She'd loved that laptop. It had contained all the papers she'd written, all her ideas for running the bookstore when she took it over. She wouldn't be able to replace those. She'd typed them up so she wouldn't have to remember them. She turned the desk chair upright and sat down on it, tears falling once again. Frustrated, she brushed them away. What a stupid thing to cry about. Sighing, she started making a garbage pile in the middle of the bed.

Craig was furious. Whoever had broken in had gotten a key. The lock had been intact. He'd have noticed if it wasn't. After determining that whoever it had been had gone, he stomped into the lobby area to confront the clerk.

The pimply, teenage desk clerk had no idea what he was in for. He sat there on his stool, bent over the day's crossword puzzle in the Star Tribune. When Craig ripped it out of his hands, he fell off the stool. "Hey man! What's your problem?"

"Who'd you give our key to?" Craig demanded, face red with anger. "Didn't I tell you when we checked in not to let anyone in?"

"Yeah, so?" He challenged.

Craig stuck his badge in the kid's face. "I'm a cop, kid. You don't want to mess with me. Who'd you give the key to?"

The kid backed away from the counter and headed for the door. Craig grabbed him by the collar of his shirt, and flung him against the wall. "Relax, man. The guy was looking for his daughter. Showed me a picture of her and everything. He was all stressed out, man."

"You haven't even seen stressed out, *man*. Do you have any idea what would have happened if we'd been there? We'd be dead. You want that on your conscience?"

"You aren't dead, so what do I care. I just work here, man."

Once again, Craig shoved him against the wall, pulled his arm back, and barely refrained from punching the kid right in the gap between his two front teeth. Stamping down on his temper, he released the quivering kid and stepped back, mentally counting to ten. "What did the guy look like?"

"Why should I tell you anything?" The kid's voice cracked. "I oughta do a citizen's arrest for police brutality!"

Craig glared at him, taking an aggressive step toward him. "You want to see police brutality? You want to be charged with obstruction of justice by refusing to cooperate with a police investigation?"

The kid cringed, and went back behind the counter. "Fine, man. Whatever. Chill out."

"I'm chilled, man. What did he look like?"

"About six foot two, maybe two hundred pounds. Older guy with light brown hair mixed with gray. He had a picture of her, man. Said he was her old man. What was I supposed to do?"

"You weren't supposed to give him a key. Ever think of calling us?"

"You weren't there."

"Well, you're gonna have a hell of a mess on your hands when your boss sees what you let happen to that room. Gonna be a little short in the paycheck for a while."

"What! That's not my fault! You're the guest, you're responsible for any damage."

"I didn't give some stranger a key. Tough luck kid. Good luck keeping your job." Craig stormed out, leaving the kid sputtering behind him.

Janine had piled everything in the middle of the bed by the time he got back. "Don't worry about that stuff," he told her when he came in. "We've got to get out of here. Sounds like your daddy was looking for you."

"You know, I'm not even shocked that he would do this anymore." Janine looked at him with angry eyes. "I'm just shocked he didn't stick around to try to finish us off."

"Grab what's left, and let's go. We'll have to go on the run for a while. We won't stay anywhere longer than one night. I'm gonna go call the captain." Craig stormed off to his car, dialing as he walked.

"Mulroney," Krista answered.

"They found us, Cap'n. Don't know how they did, but they found us."

"Are you hurt?"

"No, we were at a gun range all morning. Looks like it was McMillan himself that came for us. Clerk said he was all stressed out and looking for his daughter. He's gone now, though. I don't really understand what he was looking for. Shredded all the files."

"That's no big deal. They were copies anyway," Krista told him, running a hand over her eyes. "He skipped town yesterday. Should have warned you, but I didn't figure he'd find you. Sorry about that."

"No big deal," Craig repeated. "We're going on the run for a while. I'm gonna need a guarantee that all my expenses will be reimbursed. Credit cards included."

"You got it. Be careful. I don't know what kind of equipment these people have to find you."

"Got a name out of Ray yesterday, when he killed Janine's fiancé. Xavier. See what you can find out about that name when you get a chance. I'll check in later."

"Got it. Take care of yourself. And Janine. If he's handed out pictures of her, she might want to change her appearance. You might, too. Always better to be overly cautious."

"Ten-four. Talk to you later."

Krista hung up the phone, and sighed. This case was turning out to be bigger than expected. Now they had Ray McMillan tied to the murders of at least two people. He was obviously armed, dangerous, and unstable. Craig was a good cop at heart, he'd keep the girl safe. She just wasn't sure about the other guys when he found them. Man had a temper on him.

"Captain, your husband's on line one." A uniformed woman stuck her head in the office.

"Thanks, Mabel." Krista picked up the phone.

"Did Ray find his daughter?" Mark Mulroney asked anxiously, without saying hello. "He was looking for her. He sounded so worried. Told me he'd filed a missing person's report and everything."

Krista closed her eyes. "Tell me you didn't tell him the name of the motel where Craig took her, Mark."

"Why?" Mark sounded confused.

"He's a drug dealer and a murderer, Mark! You want to be responsible for the deaths of his daughter and one of my best detectives? How'd you even find out?"

"They were talking about it when I stopped in at your office yesterday. You can't really believe that about Ray, can you? He's always been a real stand-up guy. You know I've been friends with him forever."

"Mark, I not only believe it, I've got proof. You keep your nose out of this or I will personally arrest you for aiding and abetting a known felon. You understand?" Krista was standing behind her desk now, seething.

"All right, all right. I was just trying to help. It's his daughter, for Chrissake. See you when you get home." He hung up.

Sometimes the man drove her crazy. Well at least she'd figured out how Ray had found them. Hopefully she had put a stop to that. She really didn't want to arrest her own husband, but if he broke the law, he got the same treatment as the rest of the world.

Craig met Janine halfway across the parking lot and hurried her into the car. "I think we'll head back toward Pineville."

"Are you sure that's a good idea?" Janine furrowed her brow.

"Well, the way I see it, they won't expect us to be close by. So really, we're probably safer near Pineville than further away. Plus, then we can check out those bookstores. Do you remember which ones we wanted to look into?"

"Yes. I suppose that makes sense."

"Oh, and the Captain thinks it'd be a good idea for us to change our appearances." Craig stomped on the gas and squealed out of the parking lot, feeling a little sorry for the teenage clerk.

"Why?"

"Well, your dad had a picture of you, and I'm sure he's not the only one."

"All right. I guess I need a new look anyway since nothing else is the same."

"Good way to look at it. We'll hit Target again so we can get some clothes and stuff, and then we'll find another motel or something."

"Could we find a slightly nicer one this time? Maybe with two beds and room service?"

"Why not. I'm being reimbursed. We can stay at the most expensive hotel there is for all I care."

"Sounds good to me. I have money, too, you know."

"We'll hit a Target or something near here so you can use your credit cards, but I wouldn't do it anymore after that. Who knows if these people can trace them."

"I need a new laptop. Is there a Best Buy around here?"

"Hell if I know. If we see one, we'll go."

"How about a JC Penney's? I'm not particularly fond of Target's clothes."

"What do I look like, a fricking chauffeur?"

Janine laughed. "Sorry. A girl has a right to be picky."

"Well, great, we'll just spend the day on a damn shopping spree. Nothing else to do."

By evening, they had everything they needed for several days on the run. Janine was the proud owner of a newer, better laptop and a newer, larger backpack to carry it in, plus a nice small Penney's wardrobe. Her credit cards were much worse for the wear. She also had her very own holster to carry Craig's spare gun in, courtesy of the police department. She'd be buying her own gun when her life got back to normal, if it ever did.

They settled on a Holiday Inn in St. Paul, within walking distance of Johnson's Books, and a short drive from Bailey's Books in Forest Lake.

Janine very much enjoyed room service for dinner that night. She went to the hotel's salon when she was finished, and ruthlessly agreed to let the stylist chop off her hair. With shoulder length strawberry blonde hair, she looked different enough, and not half bad either. Sure she may have shed a few tears as at least a foot of blonde hair fell to the floor, but the old Janine was gone forever now. Maybe she'd start having people call her Jan.

Nah, that was way too Brady Bunch.

When she walked back into the hotel room, Craig almost didn't recognize her. He felt a pang at the loss of all that pretty blonde hair, but she actually looked better that way. She left California valley girl way behind with those new looks. Catholic school girl could still work. Only now she was Catholic school vixen. Craig blocked that fantasy as quick as he could once again. "You look pretty good."

"Thanks. Try to hold back on the flattery, it gets me all stirred up." She sent him a nasty look over her glasses.

With a crooked grin, Craig held out the ring he'd bought at a nearby jewelry shop. It was a simple gold band- gold-plated at least.

"Why Craig, we've only just met." Janine blinked at him, her voice dripping with sarcasm.

"Shut up. It's part of our cover. I figured no one would look twice at a married couple. Mine matches."

"Isn't that lovely. You really shouldn't have spent so much."

"Whatever. Just put it on."

She shoved the cheap band on her left hand, and thought of the two carat princess-cut diamond that had sat just there a few days before. Back when her life was normal. She shook off the melancholy mood and glanced back at Craig. "Don't you think people will find it a little odd for a married couple to be renting a room with two beds?"

"Maybe we want a little variety in our sex life." Craig sent her a wicked smile.

"You're sick. I'm sorry that you think that would be variety." She skimmed her gaze over him, and noticed he looked exactly the same. "Aren't you changing your appearance?"

"Yeah. Tomorrow I won't shave."

"Wow. Try not to put too much effort into it."

"Hey, a beard makes me look completely different. I might even just go with a mustache and sunglasses. Beards are itchy. Strawberry blonde isn't all that dramatic a change from plain old blonde either, you know."

Janine rolled her eyes and dug her laptop out of her new bag. "Whatever. I'm going to research Johnson's and Bailey's books a little before we head there tomorrow if that's all right with you."

"Suit yourself."

The rest of the evening passed with Craig watching a movie and Janine poring over her computer. Both of them were thankful when they were able to stretch out in their own beds without having to worry about the other's comfort.

Mark Mulroney was finishing a movie of his own that evening when his phone rang. When Ray McMillan greeted him, he glanced around the house, grateful that Krista wasn't in the room. "I'm not supposed to talk to you. Krista threatened to arrest me for aiding and abetting a known felon today."

"I've got to find her, Mark. I've got to make her listen to me. You know Janine is everything to me. I can't bear to think of her getting hurt. She's left the motel, and I don't know where she's gone. You know as well as I do that Craig Turner has a nasty temper. I just don't want him using his fists on my daughter."

"Ray, is what Krista is telling me true? Did you murder someone?"

"You know I could never do such a thing, Mark. I can't believe you'd even ask. I'm being framed. I got wrapped up in a bad situation with bad people, and now I'm being framed. You believe me don't you?"

Mark could hear the pain in his old friend's voice. "Look. Don't call me anymore. If I figure out where Janine and Detective Turner are, I'll let you know. I've got your cell phone number. I can't risk Krista finding out that I'm helping you. I believe you, Ray, and I'll help if I can, but try to keep out of trouble. I don't want you getting hurt, either."

"Thank you so much, Mark. You're the only person I can trust. The only friend I've got left. Let me know as soon as you hear anything."

"All right. Take care now, Ray."

Mark hung up the phone, feeling guilty for lying to his wife. She had to be wrong in this case. His wife was a brilliant woman, but even she made mistakes sometimes. There was no way Ray was a drug dealer, let alone a murderer. A man had a right to see his own daughter. Mark knew about Turner's poor treatment of suspects, knew he had a bad temper, even knew why Turner's wife had thrown him out. There was no telling what a man like that might do, and until Krista provided Mark with the proof she claimed to have, he was going to make sure Ray knew his daughter was safe. If he had children, he knew Ray would have done the same for him. After all, that's what friends were for.

Chapter Eight

Johnson's Books was a narrow brick building squeezed into a row of similar buildings in downtown St. Paul. It was considerably smaller than McMillan's Booksellers, and hadn't been in business nearly as long. Janine and Craig strode in, Craig now sporting both a slight mustache and the beginnings of a beard, and Janine immediately began asking the clerk behind the counter where she might find the romance section. She fluttered her eyelashes and flirted with the young man as if she'd been doing it forever. The clerk led her to the far end of the store, leaving the front empty, since there weren't very many customers this early on a weekday.

Craig took the opportunity to push through an 'employees only' door, in the hopes of finding something in the storeroom. He walked along the room as quietly as possible, straining to hear if there was anyone present. When he had determined that all was quiet, he worked his way over to a number of palettes stacked against the wall.

Since they still had yet to determine which books were most likely used for the drug trafficking, he began to dig through the palettes as randomly as he could. It didn't help that there were usually several titles stacked together on the same palette.

After poking holes in plastic wrap at random for about an hour, Craig had to assume the store was clean. At least, they weren't as active in their sideline as McMillan's was. If they had been, he was sure he would have found something.

Satisfied, he eased open the door and peered back into the store. Janine stood at the front counter, still busily chatting up the clerk who was all but drooling over her. Craig chuckled to himself when he noticed the pile of books the clerk was stuffing clumsily into a white plastic bag. He had left her to browse for quite a while, and of course she'd found some books she couldn't live without. She was a bookworm through and through.

He grabbed a book at random off the self-help shelf, and strode to the counter. Happily keeping up their cover, he put his arm around Janine's waist and kissed the top of her head. To her credit, she barely even grimaced. "All finished, honey?"

"I sure am, dear. Did you find what you were looking for?"

"Sure did." Finally, he glanced at the book he had grabbed. "*Gardening for Dummies*. I need as much help as possible in that area. Looks like a good book." He handed the clerk his money, shoved the book into Janine's already overloaded bag, and grabbed her hand to pull her out of the store.

The second they were out, Janine yanked her hand out of his grip, determinedly ignoring the reaction the contact had caused. To spite him, she wiped her hand off on her shorts as if she had touched something nasty. "*Gardening for Dummies*? You couldn't have grabbed some financial book or something a little more appropriate for you?"

"Jeez, it's not like I looked at the cover."

"Well, from the shape your garden was in at your house, maybe it will do you some good." She smirked. "Find anything?"

"No. It'd help if we had an idea which books were ordered most often."

"So, shouldn't you have gotten a warrant to do that or something?"

"I'll get a warrant when I know which store is Ray's supplier. Why disturb the judge for nothing? As long as we have some other way to connect the stores, it shouldn't be a problem getting one when we need it. Anyway, I don't think that store's the one."

"Why not?" They began walking back toward the hotel. Janine closed her eyes and raised her face to the morning sun. It was a beautiful summer day.

Barely, Craig resisted taking her hand again. "Too small. I did as random a search of those palettes as I could and I didn't find anything suspicious. They had a lot of self-help books and cookbooks. It doesn't seem like those kinds of books would appeal to Ray's kind of clientele."

"That in itself could make them the ones, Craig. You don't expect the drugs to be hidden in books about drugs, right? That would be a little too obvious."

"Of course I don't. I'm just saying, I would think bestsellers or something would be the best kind of books to use because so many people buy them. They wouldn't stand out."

"Webster's dictionary isn't exactly a bestseller."

"Why not? Most people own one."

Janine nodded. "You have a point."

As if on cue, Craig's cell phone rang. "Turner."

"Mulroney. I've had quite the group of cops poring over McMillan's files all night, and I think we've come up with some likely books he might use for trafficking. Care to hear them?"

"Let 'er rip, Cap'n. That would really help my investigation."

"We picked *Catcher in the Rye*, *One Flew Over the Cuckoo's Nest*, *Webster's Dictionary*, Stephen King's *Cujo*, Betty Crocker cookbooks, a couple of various topics for Dummies, Dean Koontz's *Lightening*, and the Harry Potter books for a start. They were most frequently ordered, and shipped out the farthest. Those were the criteria we were going by, so hopefully that will give you an idea. Did you get all those?"

Craig listed them off to Janine, who had pulled a mini notebook out of her bag. "Got 'em. Seriously? Harry Potter?"

"Popular books right now for adults as well as children."

"That's kind of sick. Any other ideas?"

"We suspect he switched the titles around a lot. There are rather suspicious sales on certain titles, including a thesaurus. We haven't figured out how the customers identified themselves as potential buyers. Maybe you could ask around in the ghetto, see if you can get any information off the locals."

"We're heading up to Forest Lake this afternoon to check out Bailey's Books as a potential supplier, but we'll ask around. Just came from Johnson's Books, didn't see anything suspicious there. I didn't see a lot of any of those titles there except for the Harry Potter series, and the ones I checked were clean."

"Why are you looking at the smaller stores?" Krista asked.

"Janine figured the supplier would be unlikely to be a…what did you call it, Janine?"

"Wholesaler."

"Yeah, a wholesaler. They're the ones that ship to the whole country all the time. So we're looking into individual distributors. Right?" Janine grinned at him and nodded.

"Whatever you think is best. Ask the locals to see if you can get anything out of them. Don't be afraid to bribe them."

"It's your dollar. I'll check in later. Thanks for the help, Captain." He hung up, stuck the phone back into his pocket and turned to Janine. "Looks like we get to go explore the ghetto this morning. Can you handle that?"

"Sure, as long as I get to hold one of your guns."

"You got it. Let's go back to the hotel. That way you can put away your new library, and we can take the car out to the projects. We'll pack up and head to another hotel this evening. Sound good?"

"Sure thing, boss. Are you sure you want to bring your shiny Mustang into the depths of despair?"

"We may need a quick getaway."

"You know, for a cop, you're kind of a scaredy-cat. It's not like it's the middle of the night. I don't go anywhere near that area at night."

"It's always best to be prepared for the worst."

"That's an excellent philosophy. Too bad I didn't know it sooner." Janine frowned.

"You're holding up pretty well, actually. Compared to the blubbering mess you were when I picked you up."

"I'm handling it. As long as I don't think too hard about everything that's happened, I can maintain." She sent him a small smile. "Shit happens."

"True enough. You're tougher than I thought you were, Janine."

Janine stopped in her tracks and stared at him in mock disbelief. "I think that's the first compliment you've given me. I didn't think you had it in you." Despite herself, she was touched, but he didn't need to know that.

Rolling his eyes, Craig held the door open when they reached the hotel. He admired the view as she marched toward the elevator. The girl wore shorts very well. He even liked the sexy swing of her reddish blonde hair. Come to think of it, there wasn't a whole lot he didn't like about Janine now that she'd finally stopped bawling. She was tougher than he'd thought. Another woman would still be hiding in a hole somewhere waiting for her life to put itself back together. Here she was, helping him in an investigation to prove that her own father was guilty of murder and part of a drug ring. He hadn't even seen a single tear glisten in her eye lately. It was a definite improvement. Unfortunately for him, strong women were his weakness. That's why he'd fallen for his ex-wife. Any other woman wouldn't have had the guts to toss him out.

After a quick lunch, they headed out to the ghetto. Janine felt a little odd wearing a holster and toting a gun, but the light zipped up sweatshirt she threw over them hid them well enough. A breeze had picked up, so it was a little cool in the shade from the buildings. At least the sweatshirt wouldn't look suspicious. Craig had tucked his gun in the waistband of his jeans and tugged his tee shirt down over the lump it made. He was much too manly for a sweatshirt.

Janine hung back when they came to an alley in which several likely looking men were hovering. She wasn't fond of the cities, and especially not this area. The gun was a comfort.

Craig strode casually up to the group, bummed a cigarette, and exchanged some small talk about the weather. When he felt that they had accepted him somewhat, he broached the subject. "Any of you guys know where a guy like me could find a little pick me up?"

"You a cop, man?" One of the men asked, his hand slipping into his sweatshirt pocket in a way that made Craig uneasy.

"Hell no, man. Just wondering where a guy could find a can of Coke around here, if you get my meaning."

"What makes you think we'd know anything about that?"

"Twenty bucks says you might know a little bit about this Internet ordering I've heard a rumor about. Couldn't be that easy, could it?" He held out the bill and watched the man's eyes look at it hungrily. "I heard you can get it delivered right to your home and everything. Sounds like a hell of an idea."

Another member of the group piped up, snagging the twenty out of Craig's hand. "I might have heard of something like that. I'll share it with you if you swear you ain't no cop."

"I'm no pig, man. Just curious."

The man grabbed Craig by the sleeve of his shirt and led him to the end of the alley as if he didn't want his buddies to hear what he had to say. "My brother knows a guy that gets the shit that way. It's incredible, man. Me, personally, I'm not into that shit."

"I'm sure you're not," Craig nodded.

"Here's how it works. You find out about it by word of mouth, so I'm doing you a favor. Another twenty and I'll tell you everything I know."

"How about you tell me everything you know, and then I give you another twenty. Just in case you're trying to sell me a sack of shit."

"I get ya, man. Sounds fair." He sized Craig up, and nodded. "So my brother's friend gave me this card with a number on it. Told me to go to a website for McMillan's Booksellers, pick out any book that looked interesting, and enter this number in the promotional box on the checkout page. You followin' me?"

"Yeah. Any book you wanted?"

"Any book, man. So I tried it. Like an instant later, I get an instant message from this guy named Ray thanking me for being a first time customer and some such shit, and a phone number. Says for the best deal you can get in books, call this number. So I do. Guy answers and asks where I got the number, and I tell him. He says my brother's friend's one of his best customers. Asks me the code word he gave me as extra proof. He asks me what book I'm looking for. I tell him a book with a little something extra and he totally tells me how I can get coke sent right to me. Doesn't say it like that, covering his butt and all, uses a bunch of other happy phrases, but I get the picture. He says all I gotta do is buy a book off the website and pay just for the book with my credit card. Then he fills me in on how the book don't ship until he receives the cash for the something extra. Says it's gotta be cash. Tells me where to drop it off and when. All anonymous like, man. He doesn't see me, and I don't see him. I get the cash together, do like he says, and like, three days later the book arrives in the mail with a little extra pick me up stored right inside. It's awesome, man. Unless somebody searches every package you get, there's no freaking way you can get caught. Makes me wish I owned a bookstore."

"Sounds awesome. Do you still have the card?" Craig was itching to get his hands on it.

"Yeah, I'll give it to you for the other twenty dollars. Plus the code word. He sends me a new code on the receipt every time I order, stuck on there like a coupon for ten percent off my next purchase. Nothing fishy about it. It's totally awesome, man. Slick as spit."

Craig handed over the other twenty, and the man passed him the card. "What's your name in case he asks me who I got it from?"

"Tell him you got it from Zoner. That'll do the trick."

"Thanks man, you've been a lot of help."

"No problem. Code word's Freud. Thanks for the forty, man!" Zoner gave Craig a casual wave over his shoulder and walked back to the group.

Craig laughed at the absurdity of the 'code word.' Freud had been a cocaine addict, so it was rather appropriate. He still had some questions, but at least he had the basic idea. He glanced at the card. It was a rather battered blank business card with a handwritten number on it. If a person didn't know what it was for, they'd have no way of figuring it out. It was pretty clever, really. If they had the code, they knew what it was for, so there wouldn't have been a lot of risk. Of course, he was a cop, and all he'd had to do was ask about it and he knew how the whole operation worked. But the cops had to know about it before they could ask. Who ever would have thought of a bookstore for a front, anyway?

He strolled back around the corner to Janine and passed her the card. "That was easy. Cost me forty dollars, but it was really easy. It's brilliant, really. The whole set up." He explained it to her, smiled when she laughed at the code word as well.

"That totally sounds like something my dad would have come up with. He always had a great sense of humor. Some of it still doesn't make sense, though." She climbed into the car when he held the door open. "I mean, coke addicts need coke all the time, right? So why wouldn't anyone notice if they were getting packages all the time? If you think about it, the kind of people you'd think of as being addicts probably wouldn't be really big into reading."

"Receiving packages all the time is no reason to be suspected of anything illegal, especially if they're from a legitimate source. Messing with the mail is a felony. People spend a lot of money ordering things off the Internet, especially with E-bay now. Besides, I suspect Ray probably set a limit of how many times they could order per month or something. I'd be willing to bet that whoever the sister stores are that are active in this also receive orders from the same people. That way, it's less suspicious, especially if a lot of stores share orders. It's ingenious, really. Whoever thought of this was very clever."

"There's no way my dad would have come up with a system like that on his own," Janine stated. "I'd be willing to bet big money that Xavier's the mastermind. My dad may be a lot of things, but brilliant isn't one of them."

"There'd have to be a lot of stores involved. They wouldn't all be linked to each other, either. That way if they ever got caught, it wouldn't bring the whole operation down."

"They've got to be linked somehow. I'm betting whichever store is Xavier's, it's the hub. If we brought that store down, it probably would destroy the whole operation. The only problem is, it would be really hard to pick out which are the illegal purchases. If they've got a different code all the time, the only ones we'd be able to find would be the ones who used this original code. That would be really hard to figure out."

"Except we'd know that whoever used the original code was definitely involved. After that, even with another code, they're still ordering cocaine. It would take a long time to figure that out, but it would be worth it. We'd probably fill up an entire prison."

When they walked back into the hotel, Craig took her hand without even realizing he had done so. Janine figured he was maintaining their cover, so didn't protest. She was beginning to like the sensation of their being a pseudo couple.

Glad to find everything intact when they returned to their room, Craig called the captain to share what they had discovered.

"That really is brilliant, isn't it? So there really aren't any particular books for us to follow. That'll make it tough." Krista Mulroney stated. "If McMillan has been getting away with this whole thing this long, imagine how long Xavier's been doing it."

"It'll be the bust of our lifetimes when we bring this guy down." Craig grinned into the phone. "I can't wait." And maybe, just maybe, he'd find another link in the chain of truth about what had happened to his father. This could be the very drug ring James Turner had stumbled onto years ago. It'd be a heck of a coincidence, but it was possible. How many drug rings could there be in Minnesota?

"We've still got a long way to go, Turner. Don't get your hopes up yet."

"We're on our way to Forest Lake pretty quick here." Craig glanced at the two bars showing on his cell battery. "We'll probably be at a Best Western if they have one, in case you need to find us. I don't know how much longer my phone's going to last. I'll have to pick up a charger."

"Ten-four." Krista jotted 'Forest Lake Best Western' on a post-it note and stuck it to her desk. "Maybe Bailey's Books will be the one."

"We can always hope."

"Catch ya later, Turner." Krista hung up.

"Pack your stuff, Janine. We're on the move again." Craig began throwing his things in the bag he'd bought.

Janine groaned. "Do you think we could stay at the next place for more than one night? I'm already getting tired of jumping around." She tossed her things together.

"We'll see. Get a move on." Craig flung his bag over his shoulder and went to check them out.

Janine followed shortly after and waited in the car for him, thankful that Forest Lake was less than a half an hour away. This would be the shortest trip they'd made thus far.

Or so she thought, until Craig decided to make their way to the new city in the most round about way he could think of, just in case someone was following them.

An hour and a half later, they finally pulled into the Best Western motel. Janine sighed as she climbed out, noting the time. Seven o'clock. It had still been the shortest trip they'd made, but not by much.

She tossed her bag on the flowered bedspread when they reached their room, and turned to Craig with her arms crossed. "Since you had to make that such a long trip, we're here too late to hit Bailey's today. They're only open until six o'clock during the week."

"How do you know?" Craig asked.

"I looked at their website. Store hours are posted. It wasn't hard to find. They open at ten."

"Oh, well. It's still better to be overly cautious." Craig grabbed the remote and turned on the television.

Janine sighed and sat on the bed, resigned to passing another evening doing nothing. There were no longer files to pore over, and she'd already discerned everything she could from the store websites. She glanced at the bedside table and noticed a menu. With a small smile, she pulled it toward her. At least they still had room service.

Chapter Nine

Bailey's Book was a big brick building on an out of the way street in Forest Lake. It looked very similar to McMillan Booksellers, but without the lavish landscaping.

Janine strode up to the counter and expertly distracted the clerk the same way she had in the previous store. She was learning a lot of new things about herself. She had never considered herself a master flirt, but judging from the way the young men reacted to her, she must have had better abilities than she thought. It was pathetic, really. This particular young man all but tripped over himself leading her to the mystery section.

Craig shook his head at the teenager as he walked along the back of the store, looking for the Employees Only door. Janine was gorgeous, but she wasn't *that* hot. He pretended not to notice the twinge of jealousy at the way Janine smiled and flirted with the kid. That kid had probably seen her smile more often than he had.

When he found the door, he was disappointed, but not surprised, to find it locked. Looking around for cameras or mirrors, Craig was pleased that the store's security was so bad. Of course, that alone was enough proof that this probably wasn't the store. A bookkeeper smuggling drugs out the back alleyway would be more likely to want to know who was entering the storeroom.

Realizing that he was breaking the law, as well as police protocol, he jimmied the lock open with his pocketknife. He was no master thief, but the lock was easy enough to break. Peering over his shoulder, shaking his head again as he heard Janine laugh, Craig slipped through the door.

The room was very similar to Johnson's bookstore. Palettes of books were spread all over, though in a slightly more organized fashion. Once again, he randomly poked into various plastic-wrapped piles and shook out the books. Nothing so far.

Then a realization struck. He had only been opening books along the edges. If he were going to hide cocaine in books, he'd probably hide them deeper in the stacks.

Heaving a sigh, he found a stepladder and opened the top of a palette. He pushed books aside, struggling to reach as deep into the pile as he could go without knocking books down.

Still nothing.

In the middle of searching the next palette, he heard the door open. His heart stopped. Wouldn't it be lovely if he, Detective Craig Turner, were caught digging through books in the back of a store without a warrant? Cringing at his carelessness, he squeezed himself between some palettes as he heard two people enter.

Obviously, there was more than one employee working here today. Then again, it was Saturday. He listened as the two men, teenagers again, talked about an upcoming fishing trip they were apparently both going on. How they hadn't noticed that the door had been unlocked, Craig had no idea. Teenagers.

He eased around the palettes as they walked past, heading for the door. The conversation switched to one of the boy's recent experiences with his girlfriend, and Craig had to stifle a laugh. Nope, they definitely don't appear to be drug dealers.

He reached the door and crept back out, hoping no one would see him. With a sigh of relief, he headed for the mystery section to find Janine. He groaned inwardly when he saw that once again, she had a nice pile of paperback books in her arms. Unbelievable.

At the same moment, back in Minneapolis, Mark Mulroney strode into police headquarters, barely earning a glance from the officers. He was here often enough that no one questioned his arrival. He turned his gaze toward his wife's office, guiltily pleased to see that she wasn't in it.

Under the pretense of inviting his wife to lunch, Mark waited for her in her office, surreptitiously scanning her desk for a sign of Janine's whereabouts. He really did want to have lunch with Krista. She'd been so busy with this case that she'd hardly been home except to sleep.

A little yellow post-it caught his eye. 'Forest Lake Best Western' was all that was written on it. His instincts told him this was what he was looking for. Glancing around for Krista one more time, he pulled out his cell phone and dialed Ray's number. When Ray answered, Mark thought he sounded worn out.

"Hey, pal. It's Mark. Got a little information for you." Mark said.

"Do you know where she is? Tell me!" Ray's voice was filled with desperation, and a little bit of something else.

Mark's conscience tugged at him as he realized the sound was desperation touched with madness. *No, it couldn't be. Ray was a solid, stand-up guy. He had to be imagining things.* "Yeah. Forest Lake Best Western."

Ray hung up without another word. Mark stared at his phone in wonder. What had he done? That wasn't the way a concerned father would have reacted. He slipped the phone in his pocket and turned around.

Krista was standing in the doorway, a look of shocked disbelief on her face. "How could you, Mark? Do you have any idea what you may have done? He'll *kill* her, Mark! He's not the same man anymore! Don't you realize that?"

All at once, Mark felt riddled with guilt. He'd betrayed his own wife. Then fear broke through as he watched her take out her handcuffs. The look of disbelief was replaced with anger, the like of which he'd never seen on her face. "What are you doing?" he gasped as she walked toward him.

"I warned you, Mark. You have just aided and abetted a felon right in front of me! You're going to jail." She slapped the cuffs on him and dragged him across the office toward the holding cells, reciting his rights as she went. She ignored his cries, begging her to reconsider what she was doing. Shame burned her face as she shoved her very own husband into a cell. Without so much as a backward glance, she walked away.

Mark sat on the bench, numb with shock. His own wife had just tossed him in a cell. He was going to prison. If only he could undo what he had done. But it was too late. He laid back on the bench and stared at the ceiling in disbelief.

Krista marched back into her office and slammed the door shut. Hopefully he'd learned his lesson. Despite her best intentions, she couldn't press charges against her own husband. She couldn't toss him in jail for believing in a friend. She needed him too much.

Furiously, she brushed a tear away, knowing it was a sign of weakness, and sat rigidly at her desk. He didn't need to know he wasn't going to prison. She'd let him think about what he'd done. Turner would protect Janine. He had damn well better. If Janine died, Mark was going to prison whether or not Krista needed him.

For now, he'd damn well sit in that cage and rot until this investigation came to a close.

Krista picked up her phone and called the Best Western to warn Craig. To her dismay, he was apparently renting a room under an assumed name. He'd forgotten to tell her that part. Clever boy. She called his cell phone and left him a message, confident that he'd receive it.

In another office, not so far away, one person overheard the conversation between Mark and Ray that no one had expected. Xavier had long since tapped Ray's phone.

With the girl's new location now known, and knowing that Ray McMillan was too weak to dispose of his own flesh and blood, Xavier turned on the voice distorter and sent two men after her, and two more after Ray. This time, they had better finish the job, or Xavier would personally be taking over this particular battle.

When the red phone rang, Ray was on the line. Xavier smirked. "Hello, Raymond."

"I've found her, Xavier. I'll take care of her. You don't need to send anyone else." Ray sounded desperate.

"What makes you think I would, Raymond?"

"I know you don't think I can't do it. But I can. I swear."

Xavier clucked. "It's too late for you, Raymond. You've had enough time. I'm taking matters into my own hands now. I suggest you find somewhere to hide."

"You're after *me*? What for?" Ray's voice was terrified now.

"You're a loose end. I snip loose ends. The police are after you. If they find you, you'll ruin everything. Consider your life over, Raymond. Goodbye." Xavier hung up with an evil laugh.

Janine smiled at Craig when he joined her near the bookshelves. "Sorry. Bookworm." She nodded to the books in her arms.

"How do you even find time to read all these books?" Craig asked, smiling back.

The clerk caught the chemistry between them, and slumped away like a scolded puppy. Why were the good ones always taken? Whatever. She was probably too old for him anyway.

"I have a lot of time right now," Janine pointed out. "I read for an hour and a half last night while you watched *Army of Darkness*."

"You didn't like that movie? It's hilarious!"

"Yeah. Zombies are always funny." Janine rolled her eyes and continued studying the titles on the shelf.

"You don't like movies?" Craig was shocked. There was no hope for a relationship with this woman if she didn't like movies.

"Of course I like movies. *Good* ones. I like dramas, most comedies, romance movies...all kinds of them. Sometimes I just prefer to read."

Craig breathed a mock sigh of relief. "You had me worried there for a moment."

"Anyway," She lowered her voice. "Find anything?"

"No. This isn't the place either." He scanned the titles himself. "I could pick out a good book for you if you want to try your hand at using your brain."

"Funny. Let's get out of here." Craig grabbed her hand again and strode toward the register.

"I'm not done looking!" Janine cried indignantly.

Craig stopped and turned to face her, glancing at her stack of reading materials. "You're already holding seven books. There won't be any room left in your bag if you keep this up."

Janine sighed. "I suppose you're right. It'll take me a month to read all the ones I've already picked out."

Craig laughed at her obvious disappointment. She looked like he'd broken her heart. Her lush lips were dipped into a pout, her brown eyes sulky. Once again possessed by some unpredictable demon dedicated to making his life miserable, Craig was forced to kiss her.

He felt her body stiffen at first as if to resist. What was meant to be a light kiss suddenly blossomed into much more than that. Seconds later, she melted against him. Sliding his hand beneath her hair, he dipped her head back and deepened the kiss.

Janine's heart beat a tarantella in her chest. Her blood heated close to boiling, and her mind shut off. His kiss brought out feelings in her she knew she'd never felt before, feelings she wanted to go on feeling forever. With desire overwhelming her, she didn't even notice as her stack of books fell to the floor. Her arms banded around him like iron, her body pressed to his in a subconscious desire to make them one.

That damn demon was dangerous. Craig could feel every particle in his body yearning to press her up against a bookshelf and take what he longed for.

Then he realized where they were. They were slobbering all over each other in a public place. Gathering his strength, he pulled away from her. The look in her eyes made him want to grab her by her hair and drag her back to his cave. Her eyes were dark with newly discovered passion, her lips were soft and full, bruised from his. The clerk eyed them enviously from the counter, his Adam's apple bobbing.

Straining for some control, Craig pushed her away from him. The passion in her eyes vanished, replaced by flames of fury and hurt.

"You bastard." She whispered. Face red with shame, she bent to gather her books. Leaving Craig standing there, she hastily paid the clerk the money and left the shop.

Craig's brain finally clicked back on. Now he'd done it. He raced after her, reaching her just as she opened the car door. She saw him, slammed it shut again, and rounded on him, eyes blazing.

"How dare you treat me like that," she shouted. Her finger dug into his chest as she poked him repeatedly, emphasizing each word as she continued. "Do you think I'm just some toy you can play with for your pleasure? *No one* makes me feel the way you just did, then shoves me away as if I were trash!"

Craig held his hands up in defense. "Whoa! I didn't mean it!"

"You didn't mean it? *You didn't mean it!*" She drew back her arm without even thinking and slapped him. Shocked by what she'd done, scared of the anger on his face, she backed away, the rush of color instantly evaporating from her cheeks. She'd assaulted a police officer, just like Zsa Zsa Gabor.

He held a hand to his cheek, and glared at her. "Don't you *ever* do that again."

His voice was positively icy. He moved toward her, and Janine rounded toward the front of the car. She had suddenly remembered his temper. Struggling to be brave, she dared to speak again. "That's the second time you've made me feel like that. Like I'm nothing. I don't appreciate it." She continued backing down the side of the car, her voice shaking, her heart pounding.

In one lunge, he was on her. Before she could even flinch at the blow she knew was coming, he had her pressed against the driver's door, his mouth fused to hers once again.

The breath backed up in her lungs. Her arms wrapped around him, pulling him closer. The stubble of his beard set her skin tingling. His hands skimmed along her sides, caressing the sides of her breasts. She felt warmth spread through her like fire. God she wanted him.

She had never wanted anyone as much as she wanted him. It was incredible.

Then it was over.

Craig's face hovered inches above hers, his eyes dark with desire. His voice was rusty when he finally spoke. "Did that feel like nothing to you?" Janine shook her head almost imperceptibly. "You're lucky I didn't throw you down on the floor of the bookstore and finish the job." He caressed her cheek. His sudden gentleness was unnerving, and had Janine's heart turning over in her chest. "We were making out in the middle of a public place, Janine. That's the only reason I pushed you away. Believe me, sooner or later, we *will* finish this." He touched his lips to hers gently, then backed away, silently cursing his fickle heart. This was no longer just lust that he was feeling. He cared about her more than he had about any other woman in quite some time. He didn't like it, either.

Janine gradually felt her heart begin to beat again. When he stepped away from her, she felt as if she'd been burned. She staggered back around the car and climbed in the passenger side. She couldn't believe how she'd just behaved. She had embarrassed herself. The worst thing of all was that she knew Craig was right. Damn him. He'd gone and made her fall for him.

Without another word, they headed back to the motel.

Ray McMillan watched them pull up from a far corner of the motel parking lot. Mark had been right. His old friend had come through for him. He smiled at the bag he saw clutched in Janine's hands, full of books. She never could resist a good book.

She'd cut her hair off. It gave him a pang. He had loved his daughter's hair. But she was still beautiful. He admired her new strawberry blonde color, wondering if she had known that her mother's hair had been that same shade. He swallowed as he felt his throat grow tight with impending tears.

He had to go in there. He didn't know what he would do when he did, but he had to. He still couldn't kill his own daughter. It didn't matter what Xavier said.

He would kill the cop and take her with him. She needed protection from both the detective and Xavier's men. He was the only one that could save her. She had to understand how much he loved her. How much he needed her.

They would go to Mexico and spend the rest of their lives in leisure, just him and his Neeny. They could go fishing together, camping, open a new bookstore in Mexico. They both spoke Spanish. They'd be able to do it. He had plenty of money.

She would understand why Turner had to die. Why Brian had needed to die.

He opened the door of the car, and had placed one foot on the ground when he saw them come back out. They got back into the Mustang and drove off.

Delighted that they had given him the opportunity, Ray broke into their room and waited for them to return. Nervously, he glanced at the shiny gun in his hand and imagined what it would do to Detective Craig Turner's body.

Lunch began with an awkward half hour for Janine. She picked at the salad she had ordered, barely tasted her French Dip sandwich. She was still riddled with guilt about the way she had behaved. Finally, when she could stand it no longer, she took a deep breath and looked across the table at Craig. "Look. I'm sorry I slapped you. I shouldn't have reacted that way."

Craig glanced up from his cheeseburger and smiled at her. "That's all right. It's not a big deal. I understand how you felt. That was the second time I had hurt your feelings, and I'm sorry, too. Just don't ever do that again."

Janine felt instantly better. "Believe me, I won't." She bit her lip. "I've never slapped anyone before. It felt pretty good."

"I didn't think so," Craig said through a mouthful of burger.

Janine laughed and dug into her food with a renewed appetite. "You're a pretty nice guy, Craig. Did you know that?"

"You noticed? I need to do a better job of hiding it."

Janine giggled. It wasn't so bad to be in love with him. He had a good sense of humor, had always been honest with her, and had better control over his temper than people thought. He'd have slapped her back if he didn't. She would have deserved it, too.

He was a good cop, Janine thought as she delved into her salad. He would help her find justice for Brian, of that she could be sure. So far, he had proven that he could be trusted, and that was the most important thing in the world to Janine.

How would Brian have felt about her feelings for Craig?

Janine herself was amazed that it had only taken a matter of days for her to fall in love with him. But here she was. She had felt a different kind of love for Brian, and wondered if their marriage would even have lasted. Deep down, she knew it wouldn't have worked. Brian hadn't had enough ambition, and Janine knew that would have turned her against him eventually. But he had been a great man. Weak, but great.

He hadn't fought for her when she'd left him. He hadn't chased her down and begged her to come back. Would it have made a difference if he had?

No. The betrayal Janine had felt from him had been far too strong. She only hoped that he understood that she had loved him with all her heart up until that moment. She still loved him. She hoped he would be happy for her in regards to Craig.

Her budding love for Craig was very different. She had never felt this chemistry between herself and Brian. She'd never had so much fun simply interacting with Brian, either. She knew that once she and Craig followed through on what that kiss had promised, and they would, there would be no turning back.

She could imagine what it would be like. Smoldering passion and heat, driving desire that never faltered. If that was possible. She felt her cheeks flush with anticipation.

"Where did you go?" Craig asked from across the table.

Janine jumped, face burning. "Nowhere. Just thinking." She turned her attention back to her food. Good Lord. She'd been practically fantasizing about him over French Dip and salad. Ridiculous.

Craig grinned at her. He had a pretty good idea what she'd been thinking about. A woman only looked like that for one reason.

Chapter Ten

When they returned to their motel room a short while later, Craig saw that the lock had been broken. He pushed Janine aside, and pulled out his gun.

"Stay here," he ordered her quietly.

Nudging the door open, Craig went in low, sweeping his gun from side to side. The room was intact, and none of their things appeared to have been touched. There was no sign of anyone. Standing, Craig crept toward the closed bathroom door. His breath caught in his lungs as he felt the muzzle of a gun pressed against his spine.

"Don't move, Turner," Ray McMillan spoke from behind him. "Drop the gun."

Mentally kicking himself for not looking behind the door, a very rookie mistake, Craig complied, tossing his gun on the bed, out of reach of both of them. "What do you want?"

"I want my daughter. I want to make sure you never lay a hand on her." Ray pressed harder into Craig's back, ready to shoot.

"Daddy!" Janine cried from the doorway. "What are you doing here?"

Ray smiled as he pointed the gun at her, his blue eyes slightly crazed. "Saving you, Neeny. I told you he was dangerous. Now get over here next to him." He directed her into the room with the gun.

Tears fell from Janine's eyes as she dealt with seeing her father face to face for the first time since she had fled from the bookstore.

"He's not dangerous, Daddy. He's never done a thing to hurt me." She wiped at her eyes, then held her hands behind her back.

"Maybe he hasn't yet, Neeny. But he will. I know his kind." Ray turned the gun back on Craig as he caught a movement from the corner of his eye. Craig had inched closer to the bed, trying to reach his gun. "Another move and you're dead, Turner."

When Janine stood next to Craig, Ray passed the gun from face to face. "It's all your fault, you know." His voice broke and rose several notches as he spoke to them. "It's your fault Xavier's after me, now. Both of you! If you would have just believed me, Neeny, none of this would have happened! We'd be in Mexico right now, opening a new bookstore. A clean bookstore."

"Daddy," Janine began.

"*Shut up*! Don't even talk to me. I don't even know you anymore. My daughter loved me. She would have trusted me. She wouldn't have made me have to kill Brian, or go on the run from the law. She never would have called me by my first name. I was everything to her." He swallowed as tears shone in his pale blue eyes. "I have to kill you, Neeny. That's what Xavier wants. It's the only way to save myself."

"I can't believe that you would choose yourself over me, Daddy. I never knew that about you. I never knew you could kill someone you thought of as a son. I never knew a lot of things about you. I don't know you either."

"Stop talking to me! You interrupt me again, and he's dead. I can tell you have feelings for him. What would Brian think about the fact that you're screwing a defective cop? What would he think? Is that what you are? A whore? Hiding out in motel room after motel room, spreading your legs while I'm running for my life? You could replace the man you loved in less than a week, without even a thought for the man who died for you!"

"He didn't die for me, Ray! You killed him. You did that." Janine shouted back, tears flowing freely, despite her best efforts. That he could even think that of her was just another wound to an already bruised and battered heart. She wanted to hit him. She wanted to whip out the gun at her back and shoot him right in his hideously demented face.

"Don't. Call. Me. Ray." Her father spoke each word in a voice as cold as ice. He pointed the gun at her face. "I'll kill you. I'll kill you." He muttered it over and over as Janine stared down the barrel of his gun, as if willing himself to do it. "I'll kill you. I have to kill you, Veronica. I'll kill you."

Janine shivered as Ray called her by her mother's name. He truly was insane. He was completely, and utterly wacko. Something in his brain had snapped, and there was no longer even the slightest trace of the happy, confident man who had raised her. Feeling pity for him despite herself, she hardened her heart to him. She let the loathing she felt for him rise to the surface of her emotions, suffocating all other thought. Determined to wear him down, struggling to be brave, sure that he couldn't go through with it, she kept her gaze fixed on his.

Craig watched Ray's face as he repeated the words. He could see Ray's expression moving from anger to fear, to sadness, and back again. After one long moment, Craig knew that Ray wouldn't be able to do it.

Seizing the moment, Craig tackled him and knocked him to the ground. The gun flew out of Ray's hand, and both men struggled after it. Ray slid across the ground toward the gun, and Craig pulled him back. Kicking and punching at each other, they crept closer to where it lay. Just as Ray's fingers brushed the cool metal, he froze at the voice that spoke behind him.

"Another move and you're dead, McMillan." Janine's voice was cold as she spoke.

Shocked, Ray turned to find his own daughter pointing a gun at him. He sputtered as he saw the pure hatred in her eyes. "Neeny...." He whimpered. "I love you."

"You're already dead to me, Ray." Janine replied.

With an angry wail, Ray leapt to his feet and bolted for the open door of the room, his gun forgotten.

Without a thought, Janine fired. The shot rang through the room, echoing in the tiny space. Her breath froze in her chest.

She missed. Her shot hit the doorjamb as Ray barreled through. She fired again, and missed.

"I've got him! Stay here." Craig flew to the gun on the floor as Janine ceased fire, not even bothering to stand as he fired his first shot. Ray continued to run across the parking lot, apparently uninjured. Craig raced after him and shot again, sardonically pleased as he heard Ray cry out with pain, saw him clutch his shoulder.

Ray howled and dove inside his car, careening out of the parking lot as Craig fired another shot into the rear window, and finally driving out of range.

Craig kicked the door furiously. "Dammit, he got away. Son of a…" he continued in a torrent of foul language the likes of which Janine had never heard before.

Gingerly, Janine sat on the edge of the bed as Craig continued his tirade, staring at the gun in her hand. She hadn't killed him. Was this really disappointment that she felt? She could feel the adrenaline rushing through her, suffused with anger, and she was indeed bitterly disappointed that she hadn't killed her own father.

When she'd pointed that gun at him, she had been filled with such hatred for the man that she had wanted to kill him. Oh, how she had wanted to kill him. Did that make her just like him?

She didn't have time to finish the thought as she heard the squeal of tires and another loud oath from Craig as two more cars pulled into the parking lot of the Best Western. "I have a bad feeling about this," Craig said as he shut the door all but a crack. "Get your stuff, Janine, I think we'll be making a quick escape out the back window."

She shook herself out of her trance and threw what little she had into her bag, doing the same for Craig. Within a few seconds, she stood in the bathroom, struggling to open the small window. "What's going on?"

"Looks like Xavier's found us now." Craig flung the deadbolt into place, not that it would help, and followed Janine, closing the door behind them. "Get a move on, sweet cheeks. These guys have machine guns."

Janine swore as she dragged herself through the window, trying to ignore the feel of Craig's hands as they pushed on her bottom. He was out a second after she was, and they ran to the end of the line of rooms, edging toward their car.

"We're going to have to do this right, Janine." Craig whispered, his breath hot on her ear. "As soon as they go in the room, you run for the car. I'm going to slash their tires so they can't follow us. You pick me up. Got it?"

"Got it."

"We've probably got less than thirty seconds before they figure out we're not there. I turned on the shower to throw them off." He watched as the four men approached the door. "Ready?"

Janine nodded, keys in hand.

The men kicked open the door, and stalked inside. "Go!" Craig urged, taking off.

Janine ran as fast as she could, relieved when she made it to the Mustang. She turned the key, and backed up as quickly as she could without screeching the tires. Within a few seconds, Craig was back in the car and they were on the road again. Craig watched through the back window as the men came out of the room. "Step on it, Janine!" He yelled as he watched them take aim.

Janine peeled off around a corner, and floored it back toward the highway, her heart pounding, half expecting to hear a bullet crash through the window at any moment.

Finally, they were safe. She breathed a sigh of relief. "Well that was fun."

"Oh yeah, loads." Craig smiled sarcastically at her. "Don't worry, they won't be going anywhere unless they've got four spare tires. Besides, someone had to have reported gunshots, and the police should be arriving on the scene at any minute. You did good, Janine."

"You, too."

"Now pull over. You drive like a girl."

Janine laughed weakly as she pulled to the side of a frontage road. They switched sides and Janine climbed into the passenger seat as what had just transpired overwhelmed her. She looked at

Craig as he reached for his seatbelt and was simply overcome.

Craig was just reaching for the ignition, when suddenly, Janine was on him, her mouth devouring his. His heart skipped a beat, his fingers diving into her hair, as he struggled to pull her completely onto his lap. He sent the seat back with the pull of a lever, and had to stifle a moan as she straddled him, pressing them together at all sorts of fascinating points. His hands flew inside her shirt, freeing her breasts from their bonds.

Janine cried out as his calloused hand circled her breast, teasing the points until they were hard as rock. His other hand plunged inside her shorts, his fingers diving into her center. With a moan, she felt the orgasm shoot through her like fire. She needed him inside her right now.

Without removing her mouth from his, she fumbled with the snap of his jeans, tugging them down. She moaned as her hand clamped around the length of him. Tugging her shorts aside, she lowered herself onto him inch by inch as they both cried out in unison.

Craig groaned and gripped her hips like iron, his mouth replacing his hand at her breasts. Fiercely, he bit down on his own pleasure as he pressed her back and forth, urging her to take them at any speed she liked, reveling in the feel of plunging into the welcoming warmth. He thrust harder, deeper as their speed increased. He felt her fly over another crest, crying out as she did, and urged her over one last time. Their lips locked, stifling each other's cries as they flew over the final edge together.

After a long moment of holding each other, Craig finally was able to speak again. When he did, his voice was rough with passion. "Dammit, Janine. We just did it in a car in the middle of the damn day like a couple of randy teenagers."

To his dismay, Janine burst into tears, and clung to him.

"Whoa! Okay, okay! I'm sorry! It's just that I wanted better for our first time together,"Craig stuttered, afraid he'd hurt her feelings again. She was so damn sensitive.

"I was so afraid I was going to lose you back there!" Janine sobbed, planting wet kisses all over his face. "I thought he was going to kill you. I couldn't have handled losing another man I love."

The hand that had been rubbing her back stiffened, and Craig fell silent. "What did you say?" Had she just told him she loved him?

Janine looked up and saw a trace of fear in his eyes. Realizing what she'd said, and that it was probably a little too soon to say it, she mumbled, "N-n-nothing. I said I was afraid that he'd kill you." Uncomfortably, she scrambled off of him and returned to her seat, feeling suddenly very awkward at her behavior.

"I think you might have said something else, too." Craig replied, fastening his jeans and turning to face her.

Swallowing her pride, realizing he wasn't going to let it go, Janine replied, "I said I loved you."

"That's what I thought you said." Craig leaned over and grabbed the pack of cigarettes he rarely smoked out of the glove box. Lighting one up, he gazed out the window for a moment.

"Can I have one of those?" Janine asked shakily. She felt like she was in elementary school again and was waiting to hear how she'd be punished for what she'd done. When Craig nodded, she helped herself to a cigarette, and took a drag off of it with a harsh cough. Determined to play it cool, she gazed out of her window. A moment later, she heard the engine start as Craig turned the car back onto the road.

"Thank God this isn't a busy road," Craig muttered. "Imagine if someone had seen us. I'd have been arrested for Public Fornication. Wonder how I would have explained that one to the Captain." He sent her a small smile, and he heard her chuckle.

Suddenly his voice was serious as he put out his cigarette. "Look, Janine. I care about you, too." He waited until she'd looked at him. "But I'm not a good man for you to love. I'm not a good man, period."

"What makes you say that?" Janine asked quietly.

"I damn near physically abused my ex-wife, Janine. I trashed our living room, and I barely resisted punching her square in the face. Barely resisted."

"But you resisted, Craig. You didn't abuse her."

"I've never even met my son, Janine. He's thirteen years old this year."

"She won't let you. That's not your fault."

"Dammit, Janine, I just came off of suspension for punching a suspect that I was interrogating. And they only suspended me, rather than firing me, because of my father. Does that sound like the kind of man you want to be with?"

"Craig, it sounds to me like you've got a lot of pent up anger about your father's death that you have yet to deal with. I don't think you will until you find out who it was that set him up. But you are a good man, Craig. I don't care what you think about yourself, I know a good man when I see one. And I love you already, so you're just going to have to get used to it." With that, Janine put out her own cigarette, half smoked, and cranked the radio.

"What are you, a fricking shrink?" Craig called over the noise.

Janine simply ignored him, and the rest of the ride passed in silence as they made their way to the last bookstores in the area, Low Price Adventures and Rare Books and More in Minneapolis.

Chapter Eleven

When the familiar skyline of Minneapolis arose before them, Craig finally turned down the radio and pulled out his cell phone. Reminding himself once again that he needed to buy a charger, Craig dialed the captain's number.

"Where've you been, Turner?" Krista asked him upon answering.

"We had a little run in with Ray McMillan and a few of Xavier's errand boys, so we're on the move again." Quickly, he relayed the story of what had happened that afternoon.

"It's partly my fault that they found you, Turner," Krista stated guiltily. "You'll never believe what happened here. I had to arrest Mark."

"What?"

"I walked into my office to find him telling McMillan where you were staying. He saw it on a damn post-it note I left laying around. So I arrested him. I left you a message."

"Sorry. This is the first time I've checked my phone today. I'm sorry, Cap'n, that had to have been really hard for you."

"He deserved it. I'm not pressing charges on him yet." She sighed. "I just can't. But if anything happens to either of you, he'll be going to prison."

"I won't let that happen, Captain. Anyway, I was just calling to let you know that we're done with motels. We haven't had much luck with them so far. Just to be safe, I'm not telling you where we're going."

"I understand that, Turner. Good thinking."

"We've got two more bookstores to look at out here, then we're out of luck. Bailey's and Johnson's Books aren't involved, that much I know, though you probably shouldn't ask me how I know it."

"Ten-four. Keep in touch."

"Thanks, Captain. Sorry about Mark." He hung up and noticed Janine staring at him. With a grin, he asked her, "You like camping?"

Janine smiled. "As a matter of fact, I do."

"Good thing, because we'll be living off the land for the next few days."

With the earlier tension forgotten, they stopped at a sporting goods store and stocked up on camping supplies. After buying a sticker permit, they parked at a state park near Minneapolis and set up camp.

Janine was reminded again of the first time her father had taken her camping, and struggled to erase it from her mind. Then she decided that even though he was no longer the same father she'd always known, she'd keep her good memories.

The campground was fairly quiet. It was still early June, and the camping season hadn't started full swing yet. Janine immediately felt calmer surrounded by the sounds of flies buzzing, frogs peeping, and owls hooting as evening faded into night. She caught three crappies to Craig's two, and impressed him by cleaning them better than he could.

With dinner out of the way, Janine bravely sat down next to Craig and leaned her head on his shoulder, determined to get him used to the idea that she considered them a couple. To her relief, he laid an arm around her shoulder as they stared into the fire. "This was a good idea," she told him. "Camping always relaxes me, and things have been really stressful so far. Besides, I don't think anyone will find us here."

Craig glanced at her, and was startled by how beautiful she looked in the firelight. He felt a fullness around his heart that made him feel both happy and uncomfortable. "I meant what I said earlier, Janine."

"Which part?"

"Well, all of it, but I do care about you." He tipped her face to his and kissed her softly.

"I meant what I said, too, but I won't repeat it." She kissed him back, just as softly.

"I'd like to show you what I wanted our first time together to be like, Janine."

Janine smiled teasingly, "I'm ready when you are."

Craig walked over to their tent and returned with a sleeping bag, which he spread on the ground near the fire. He walked to her and held out his hand.

Appreciating the romance of the moment, Janine allowed him to help her to her feet. She wrapped her arms around his neck and pulled his mouth to hers. Soft kisses, this time, but the feelings were the same. Janine felt her heart fill with him, glad that she had told him she loved him. It made everything seem a little nicer.

Craig's hands traveled over her body gently, caressing her hair, her back, her waist, and back again. He breathed in the scent of her and was overcome with desire. She was beautiful, better in real life than any fantasy he'd imagined her in, Catholic school vixen or not. He felt her sigh as her body melted against him, surrendering to him, willing him to do with her as he wished. She was as pliant as melting wax in his arms.

Pulling apart from her for a moment, caressing her cheek in a gentleness that was unlike him, he gazed into the brandy colored eyes that he had seen display almost every emotion imaginable in the short week that they had known each other, yet still remained strong and confident. He touched his lips to hers briefly, then dipped his hands under the end of her shirt, easing it up and over her head, kissing each newly exposed area of silky skin.

Janine shivered as she felt the combined caress of his lips and the wind on her naked flesh, though her entire body slowly filled with warmth. The air felt syrupy, thick with the scent of pine and campfire as she breathed each shallow breath. Finally, his mouth returned to hers, and she feasted on his lips, content to follow wherever he led her. She stripped off his shirt, and pressed warm flesh to warm flesh, anxious to speed things along. Her fingers fumbled again for his jeans, but he guided them to his chest, pulling her closer.

"No, my love," he whispered, not aware of the words he spoke, "this time is for you."

Her heart swelled at the words, then stopped as he swept her off her feet and lowered her to the sleeping bag. The flannel warmed beneath her skin, dappled with firelight. She ran her fingers through his shaggy brown waves as he lay beside her, admiring the way the fire twinkled and danced in his chocolate eyes. "You're so handsome," she murmured as he bent his head to hers.

Craig struggled with embarrassment about the comment for a moment, but silenced her with his lips. His hand traveled down her torso, feeling each and every goose bump, pleased with the knowledge that they were not caused by coldness, but by what he made her feel. Slipping aside her bra, leaving her bare to the waist, he caressed her breasts, slowly this time, appreciating them as he had not taken the time to do earlier. They were small and firm, a perfect fit for his hands, and very sensitive. The skin here was softer than silk, scented faintly of roses and baby powder. Their peaks hardened at the kiss of the wind, calling for his touch.

Janine moaned low in her throat, turning her body toward his so she could touch as well, but once again, he gently brushed her seeking hands aside. Unable to do otherwise, she lay them flat at her side, and let herself give in to the sensations he brought to her. She watched as his head traveled down the column of her throat, shivered as he brushed his tongue over the pulse that hammered just there, her most sensitive spot. He moved down her body and she relaxed along with him. She lifted her hips as he tugged away her shorts and the last lacy barrier that stood in his way, happy that the moment of joining was soon to come.

Craig watched her as he stripped away her clothing, leaving her bare to the air, admiring the way her eyes darkened and her cheeks flushed with passion. He caressed the area along the top of her thighs, her lower abdomen, anywhere but where she wanted him to touch until he felt her tremble with need. Dipping into the heat of her, he smiled as her body bucked with a climax. Gently he stroked and soothed until he felt her tense with another.

He stood, leaving her hanging on the brink, and removed the rest of his clothing. She cried out impatiently as he knelt down again, desperate for him. He crept back up her body, claimed her mouth with his and felt her urge him into speed. He teased her ruthlessly at the spot where their bodies were nearly joined, then worked his way back down and covered her with his mouth.

Janine cried out again as an even stronger climax tore through her. She gripped the sleeping bag as if it would help to keep her on the ground, and moved her hips in an age old rhythm with his mouth. "Oh, God, Craig," she nearly whimpered. "Please."

Finally satisfied, Craig eased back up her torso, plundering her mouth and finally letting his own pent-up passion free. He lifted her hips and plunged into her with one hard thrust. He felt her clamp around him and moved at an almost painfully slow pace, enjoying each and every sensation.

Janine didn't think she could take anymore. She pistoned her hips, urging him to go faster as she felt herself flying toward the edge again. He continued on, slowly, making sure she felt every small movement, driving her nearly insane with the onslaught of sensations. When she cried out at last, he quickened the pace, driving into her even as her hips rose to meet him. They matched each other thrust for thrust in a march as old as time, each caught up in what the other could do to them. The slap of flesh on flesh and their mingled moans joined the chorus of frogs, owls, and the aria of a loon in the distance, as they drove each other toward madness. Finally, Craig felt her tightening around him, muscles urging him to let himself go, arms and legs clinging to him like vices. With one last, powerful stroke, he let himself follow her.

They drifted off to sleep in each other's arms, gazing at the stars that twinkled high above. As Janine fell asleep, she said softly once again, "I love you."

Craig felt his heart fill, and realized that despite his every effort, he loved her as well. Protecting her became a bigger priority than protecting himself. He swore to himself that someday he would see her happy again.

If he were to consider a future with her, he had to get his life back on track. He was no good for her right now. He wanted to be the kind of man that she deserved after all her troubles, and in order to do that, he needed to take Xavier down. When he had finally gotten his justice, he'd be ready. For now, he'd just keep his feelings to himself.

Early the next morning, miles away, Ray was at his wit's end. His own flesh and blood had shot him. He couldn't believe it. Of course, he certainly deserved it. Despite how Xavier would react, Ray was glad that he hadn't killed Janine. He'd never have been able to forgive himself.

Now he had to tell Xavier what had happened.

He was dead for sure. He could only hope that once he was, Xavier would leave Janine alone for good. Not that it was likely.

Already sweating, he summoned what little courage he had left, and dialed the number.

"You've failed, Raymond." The creepy voice answered.

"How did you know?" Ray felt himself begin to shake.

"I have my ways. You've failed me for the last time. I suggest you turn yourself in, Raymond. Make things easier on yourself. I won't hurt you if you do. If you don't, my men will find you, and when they do, I guarantee you'll find the experience very unpleasant."

"All right. Where do I go?" Ray swallowed fearfully. He knew it was the only way. There was the slightest chance that he might even be able to kill Xavier before Xavier killed him. Very slight.

"You aren't far from here." The voice oozed. "Follow my directions. If you aren't here within the hour, I'll send every man I have after you. Then you will die. Be a man, Raymond, if you still can."

"Fine. Give me the directions. I'll be there." He tried to keep from crying as he wrote them down.

Within the hour, as ordered, Ray found himself in front of a bookstore called Low Price Adventures in Minneapolis. He was surprised by the store's appearance. This couldn't be the hub of the money making empire he'd been a part of for so long. It was too small.

The bookstore was crammed into an area of Minneapolis not much better than the ghettos. It was a plain, red brick building, unadorned except for a single sign that advertised its name and that it had been established in 1950.

He took a moment to admire everything about the world that he would miss. The sky was a bright, clear blue without a single cloud, birds were chirping. Cars roared by, some new, some old. He closed his eyes as a gentle breeze brushed his face, and breathed in deeply the scent of the city. Taking a deep breath, he walked in the door.

The small store was completely packed with books. Shelves overflowed, tables were heaped with them, and there were even some piles on the floor. He felt momentarily comforted by the scent of the books that he had always loved, but it was only for a moment. The room was very plain. Dull hardwood floors peaked out from under countless rugs, furniture was stuffed close together, and knick knacks could be found everywhere. It distinctly reminded him of his grandmother's old house, right down to the underlying stench of mothballs.

Squaring his shoulders, he glanced toward the front counter. He blinked. There was no one to be found except for a single elderly woman manning the cash register. He shouldn't call her elderly, she was probably only fifteen years older than he was, but she looked old. She was short and pudgy, almost round, just like anyone's favorite grandmother. Her auburn hair was curled tightly around her head, speckled with gray. She wore wire-rimmed bifocals and dressed the way anyone would envision a librarian dressing. Her suit was a drab gray with a white ruffled collar, and a maroon bow tie. She looked harmless.

He had to be in the wrong place. Confused, he walked up to the counter. "Excuse me, Ma'am," he said. "I'm looking for Xavier."

Her pale, watery eyes shifted from the book in her hand and took his measure. "Certainly, sir. Follow me." She led him toward a door at the back of the room. Punching in the code, she pushed it open, and waved him through. As she closed the door behind her, Ray was enveloped in darkness.

"Hey!" he cried, surprised, about to tell her to turn on the lights. Suddenly, he was grabbed from behind and restrained. When the fluorescent lights flickered on, two very large men held him captive, pulling his arms so far behind his back that he was forced to bend over. In shock he looked at the elderly woman. He was instantly aware of the hardness he'd missed in those eyes earlier. "Who are you?"

"Hello, Raymond," the woman said in a cold, emotionless voice. "You're right on time. I bet you're surprised to see me. My victims usually are."

"You're.... a woman!" Ray stated in disbelief.

"How sweet of you to notice, Raymond. It's the perfect cover. Who would ever suspect a matronly woman to be the head of a drug smuggling ring?" Her smile faded instantly. "You've failed me, Raymond. Now I'm afraid you must pay."

"But you said if I turned myself in you wouldn't hurt me!" Ray cried, fearing for his life.

"I don't recall saying that. Why would I lie to you, Raymond?" Suddenly, her voice turned from sweet to pure evil as she ordered her men. "Do it."

She grinned maniacally as she watched her two henchmen beat on Ray. When they were finished, his face was bruised and bloody, his nose broken, along with a few ribs. The men released him and he sank to the floor, tears of pain streaming from his eyes.

"Oh, poor, poor Raymond." Xavier said in a syrupy sweet voice. "Don't worry, my dear, you won't die yet. I have plans for you."

"What kind of plans?" Ray croaked.

"I'm going to bring you your daughter, Raymond." She only grinned as Ray cried out. "You'll find out whether she begs for mercy before she dies. I'll show you how to follow orders. And when I'm done, and her lifeless young body lies on the floor in front of you, right next to the detective's, then you can die, Raymond. Don't worry. Then you can die."

Ray began to sob. "Please. Take me instead. Let her live. Please!"

"Oh, no, Raymond. You are not nearly a good enough prize for that. Meanwhile, please enjoy your stay. Your daughter will be joining you very soon now." She turned to her men. "Lock him in the shed in the back. You won't need to concern yourselves with feeding him or providing him with drink. He doesn't have that much time left."

The men dragged Ray away, his screams echoing off the walls of the enormous, soundproofed store-room. Xavier smiled wickedly to herself. Those loose ends would be tied soon enough. She suspected young Miss McMillan and her handsome bodyguard would stumble into her store later this afternoon. Meanwhile, she had several men out looking for them. They would find them, of that she was certain. Alice Xavier Price always got what she wanted.

Ray found himself locked in a lightless, nearly airless shed within minutes. Unfortunately for him, he was saner than he had been since his whole world had come crashing down around him. Tears leaked from his eyes without his noticing as his body pounded with pain the likes of which he had never felt before.

How had he let all of this happen? He had put the one person that was most important to him in the worst kind of danger possible. His daughter had been the most wonderful part of his life, and now she hated him.

"Veronica," he whispered tearfully, speaking to the woman he had loved and lost so long ago. "I'm sorry I messed up so badly. I didn't protect our baby. What must you think of me?" His sobs were filled with shame. "At least I couldn't kill her. I never could have forgiven myself. She's everything to me. I swear to you that I'll make things right between us, somehow, if she'll let me. She's all I have."

He broke down into bitter tears of self-disgust, now more afraid for Janine's life than his own. Finally, he had his priorities right again. If only there was some way he could keep her away. That evil woman had taken his phone, or he could have called Mark and had him warn his wife about what was going to happen. Now, he was completely helpless to stop it.

It was all his fault.

He let himself revel in the wonderful memories he had of fatherhood. He remembered Janine's first day of school, the first time they went camping together, how she had looked when she'd totaled her first car. He recalled the happiness on her beautiful face when she'd told him she and Brian were engaged, how happy she'd been that he had wanted to help her plan her wedding. The wedding would never take place now because he himself had taken away the only man she'd ever loved. For the first time, Ray wanted to hurt himself. If there was a way, he'd kill himself to avoid the shame of what he'd done, but there wasn't. All he could do now was hope that he could help his precious little girl.

If Xavier did succeed in capturing Janine, he swore to himself that he would do everything he could to protect her if given the slightest chance. He would give his life for his daughter without hesitation. Her life was worth so much more than his.

Ashamed and heartbroken, he cried himself to sleep.

Two days later, Xavier's back door buzzer sounded. She opened the door to find a young Hispanic man trembling on her doorstep. "Is Xavier here?" He stuttered, sweat streaming down his face.

Xavier loved the fear that her mere name brought to her employees. She grinned at the boy, and spoke softly, "I'm afraid he's not in, may I take a message for him?"

The boy's eyes darted from side to side. He took a deep breath, looking visibly relieved. "I've come to report that there's been no sign of Detective Turner or Janine McMillan, ma'am. We've searched all the hotels and motels in the area, and any other place we could think of. Could you tell him that, please, ma'am?"

Xavier's smile stayed in place as her confidence took a sharp dip. "No sign in two days? Have they vanished? Are you sure you're looking hard enough?"

"Oh, yes, ma'am. We've tried everywhere. There's no choice but to give up. We can't find them. They're gone." The boy stepped back as if to leave.

Before he knew what was happening, Xavier had attacked. She wrapped her hands around the boy's head and snapped his neck with the smile still on her face. He fell to the ground with a thump, and Xavier dusted off her hands. "*Never* say 'can't' to me." She slammed the door on his dead body, and summoned one of her men for cleanup.

Stomping back to her office as if nothing out of the ordinary had happened, Xavier felt a new sensation creeping into her mind. Fear. She sat in the black recliner behind her desk at Low Price Adventures, sipped her chamomile tea laced with brandy, and experienced the fear of losing everything she had for the first time in her life. The longer those two were on the loose, the more likely that any day now, police would come storming through her door.

Xavier slammed her cup down on the desk, barely flinching as the hot liquid stung her hand. She had never thought that anyone would figure out that her bookstore was the root of the drug smuggling business. Never! She had been so careful to make sure that she was untraceable.

How dare they make her even the slightest bit nervous. Xavier had been running this business successfully for over thirty years. She had created the idea herself, a simple librarian with a small drug habit. When the Internet had become available, things had picked up dramatically. They said that her generation didn't understand computers. Not only did she understand them, she could hack her way into almost anything. She had made her business foolproof.

On only one other occasion had it even come close to being discovered. The fact that the very same man's son was now on her trail was almost too much to bear. When her men found those loose ends, Detective Turner would die first. She would personally take responsibility for wiping out an entire family. Xavier sneered. But first she'd inform him just who was responsible for the death of his father. That moment would be a sweet one.

Then the girl. Xavier took particular pleasure in imagining what it would do to Raymond McMillan to watch his only child, his only family, suffer in front of his eyes while he watched helplessly from the sidelines. If he'd done what Xavier had asked and killed the girl, an unkind death would not have been necessary. Now Xavier intended to break several bones in the girl's body with a blunt object before giving her the release of death. Perhaps there was a way she could still make Raymond deal the final death blow. That would be priceless. She would make it happen, even if she had to duct tape Ray's fingers to the trigger.

Picking up her glass, sipping the tea, feeling the brandy burn through her chest, Xavier began to relax again. Her men would find them. Picking up the special phone, Xavier issued an order that cleared her store of all but two of her men.

Sipping her tea, kicking her feet up, Xavier tried to imagine what it would feel like to personally vanquish three more lives in the worst ways possible. She had done it numerous times before, in various hideous ways, but she had never broken every bone in a body. Grinning to herself, she imagined that she could already hear and feel the crunching of the McMillan girl's bones beneath her fingers. It was really a delightful dream. She couldn't wait to bring it to fruition.

Chapter Twelve

    Two days of hiding in the woods had both Craig and Janine feeling refreshed and ready to continue their investigation. They broke camp after yet another fish fry lunch, and loaded up the Mustang. A quick dip in the cool lake water and a little bath-time distraction later, they were ready to begin. Their plan of attack was simple: Rare Books and More first, then Low Price Adventures.
    "So what happens if neither of these stores is the one we're looking for?" Janine asked, settling into the passenger seat. She was beginning to feel more like herself now that she had dealt with her feelings toward her father. It hurt to let go of the man she had once loved, but she had already begun to heal. As a small satisfied smile flitted across her face, Janine admitted to herself that two days of absolutely fabulous lovemaking hadn't hurt, either.
    "Then we're back to square one." Craig answered, running his fingers through his damp hair. "I have a feeling one of them is the one."
    "Why's that?"
    "Call it gut instinct." He glanced over at her as they turned onto the highway. He felt a new closeness with Janine after all they had shared in the last few days. Love did that to people, he guessed. Because her opinion mattered, he let himself open up and share his most innermost thoughts with her. "Something tells me that we're following the same trail my father was all those years ago."

"Oh, Craig," she said, "You don't think that would be a little too coincidental?"

"Not really. How many huge drug rings are there likely to be in Minnesota? We're not exactly the crime capital of the world here."

"That's true, but who says the people your father were after are still doing the same thing now?" Janine slanted her body to face him, hampered slightly by her seatbelt. The fact that he was opening up to her was a good sign. He'd been fairly tight-lipped about himself so far in their relationship. She'd practically had to pry every word out of his mouth with a crowbar. "I understand how important it is to you to avenge your father's death, Craig, but you may have to accept the fact that you won't be able to."

"You say 'avenge your father's death' as if it were the Dark Ages or something."

"Well, that's basically what you want to do, isn't it?"

"It's not that I want to, Janine. I have to. The reason I became a cop was because I believe in justice. The one that killed my father got away clean, and I can't handle that." Craig's voice rose as he continued, filled to the brim with deep, inner pain. "My mother couldn't handle that, either. She wasted away after he was killed, even though she knew that being a cop's wife meant that it could happen. She didn't even last two years. Losing him broke her, Janine. It broke me, too." He glanced out the side window as if lost in thought for a moment. Janine felt tears welling up in her eyes at the thought of what it must have been like for him. "My father deserves justice. He was a good man, he believed in the good in people, and he didn't deserve to die like that. The sooner I can give him his justice, the sooner I can continue on with my life."

"You're not continuing on with your life right now?" Janine ached for him, painfully aware of the hurt in his voice that he tried valiantly to mask with anger.

"You don't understand. For the last thirteen years, I've read and re-read all of those newspaper articles until I could spout them from memory. I've followed every trail I could, and everything always leads to a dead end. I hardly spent any time with my mother before she died because I was too wrapped up in it all. I lost my wife, I lost my unborn son, and it hardly even mattered to me back then. I've never felt like I was as close to finally finding out who did this, and what really happened, as I am right now." He slammed his hand on the steering wheel, frustration ebbing out of every pore, his eyebrows tensed into an angry frown. "This case has been my whole life. Aside from the half-assed effort I put in at work on other cases, my focus is entirely on finding the person responsible. I have no life other than this. It's my obsession, and I'll never be able to go on with my life until I finish it."

"Then I hope you're right, Craig, I really do." She reached for his hand, and held it, giving it a little squeeze of support. His fingers clung to hers as if she were the only thing keeping him afloat in a storm-tossed sea of anguish.

Then the tension dropped from his body as if someone had flipped a switch, his facial expression melting from angry into determined. "I know I am. I just know it."

Rare Books and More had only just opened for the day when Craig and Janine pulled up in front of the entrance. Unlike the other bookstores, it was set on the corner in a nicer area of Minneapolis, with a yard landscaped beautifully, though closed in by a wrought iron fence. It looked as if it had been a house at some point, built like a small box as they were in the middle of the twentieth century, with the addition of a large warehouse area on the back side.

They stepped inside, intending to proceed as they had in the other two stores, when suddenly a little old man behind the front counter called out to them.

"Janine McMillan!" He shouted, his arms open wide as he dashed around the counter to greet them. He moved very quickly for the frail octogenarian that he seemed to be. In a mere moment, he was clutching Janine's hand and shaking it exuberantly. "Don't you remember me?" he asked, taking in the blank expression on Janine's face. Then he waved a hand. "Of course you don't. I haven't seen you since you were knee high to a grasshopper. Oh, your grand-pop was so proud of you. He only knew you for a year or so before he died, but he enjoyed every second he spent with you. He'd send me pictures at least three times a week. And now here you are, all grown up." He beamed at her, showing a line of teeth so perfect and white that they had to be dentures.

Janine continued to look at him blankly. "Um, I'm sorry…who are you?"

"Wilbur Munchauser." He continued to pump her hand, the thin wisps of gray on his head bobbing along with his enthusiasm. "I was your grand-pop's co-conspirator in the bookshop biz. I've done business with your pop for years."

"Oh! Okay, sure, I recognize your name now. I've probably talked to you on the phone." She sent him an easy smile, and gently pulled back her hand. Janine found his choice of words interesting, 'co-conspirator,' and noticed Craig raise an eyebrow. "How did you recognize me after all these years?"

"Your pop knew me from the good old days when he worked with your grand-pop in the store. He sent me all your school pictures, and most recently a wedding invitation with an engagement picture in it. So congratulations!" Wilbur turned his pale, cataract stricken gaze on Craig for the first time, and his smile faded. "B-but, this isn't Brian Whitman, is it?"

Janine felt her smile fade. How was she going to explain this? "Uh, no." She let her voice thicken. "Brian was….killed recently." She answered vaguely. He didn't need to know why.

"Oh, dear me! How terrible for you! How did he die? I mean, if you don't mind me asking, as an old friend. He was so young."

"Well…," Janine looked at Craig with a panicked expression.

Craig stuck out his hand. "I'm Detective Craig Turner. We happen to be here because we're investigating the circumstances surrounding Brian's untimely and unexplained death. We believe he was murdered, but we haven't any evidence as to why or who was responsible."

Wilbur shook Craig's hand considerably less enthusiastically, but eyed him with the respect reserved only for officers of the law. "That's terrible. How can I help?"

Craig took a deep breath, and decided he'd have to search this store the legal way. If Munchauser was cooperative, there shouldn't be much of an issue. "I'd like to ask you some questions, if you don't mind."

"Oh, certainly. Certainly! Come, come, you poor thing," he said, taking Janine's hand and leading her to the small living room area. He gestured her to sit on the couch. When she complied, followed closely by Craig, he sputtered again, "Let me just get you some tea and cookies. I always keep them around here in case I need them. Then we'll talk." He bustled off to the small kitchen at the back, leaving Janine and Craig alone for a moment.

"Why didn't you tell me you knew this guy?" Craig asked Janine in a whisper.

"I didn't know I did until a minute ago. I still don't really know him, I've never met him as far as I can recall. I don't think he's the one, though, Craig. He's too old, and he has been in business with our bookstore for years. I recognize his name."

"That's just why we still need to check him out. I realize he's certainly too old to be the mastermind, but that doesn't mean he's not involved." He glanced up as he watched Wilbur scurry back into the room. "Just follow my lead. Improvise."

Janine nodded, and smiled to the old man as he handed her a cup of tea. He settled his thin body beside her, handed her a picture, and patted her knee in a paternal way. "Ask away, Officer," he said to Craig.

"Detective," Craig answered automatically. He cleared his throat as the old man nodded, his eyes expectant. He might as well come right out with it. He was good at reading expressions, and his gut told him this was not his man. "We believe that Whitman was involved in smuggling drugs."

"Really," Wilbur cried out as if he couldn't believe such a thing could happen.

Craig nodded. "We believe he was killed by a fellow smuggler. We think they were sending drugs to customers through the mail, hidden inside the pages of books. Have you heard of anything like that?"

"In books? Certainly not. The true literary could never deliberately deface a book in such a way." Wilbur's thin mouth turned down as if defacing books was somehow a worse offense than smuggling drugs.

"I'm afraid that's just what happened, sir. We're investigating different bookstores in the area to see if we can figure out who was involved. Miss McMillan deserves justice for the tragic loss of her fiancé."

"Oh, I certainly agree with you, Detective, but I'm afraid I won't be of much assistance. I know next to nothing about drugs. I've never even heard rumors of such a business operating anywhere near here, not that my customers are the type that would ever participate in such a thing."

"What type of customers do you have, Mr. Munchauser?"

"I deal primarily in the rare and priceless books at my store. My customers are well-to-do, intellectual people that value books not only for their stories, but for their history as well."

"Your store is called Rare Books and More, isn't that right?" Craig pointed out. He was momentarily distracted as Janine sniffled into a Kleenex the elderly fellow had handed her. She lay what was obviously her engagement picture on the coffee table as if she couldn't bear to hold it, and was crying softly. Craig felt a strong desire to pull her onto his lap and comfort her, but that was not his current role.

"Yes, of course," Wilbur agreed. "I do sell books besides the rare ones, but they are my primary source of income. A rare book is very valuable, and quite expensive. It is purchased to be cherished. I often provided my rare books to Ray McMillan if he had a customer that was in need of one, on the condition that he refers that customer to me from then on."

"Would you mind if I had a look at your stocks?"

"No, no, no. Please, help yourself. I would prefer that you not manhandle my rare books collection, as some of them are very fragile, but the rest you may do with as you please."

Craig recalled that Janine had said earlier that even her father wouldn't damage a rare book. "That would be fine. We're not interested in sifting through the rare books."

"Good. Follow me." Wilbur led them to the back of the store and pushed open the swinging door to the storage room. He flipped on the lights and stood next to the door, waving Craig toward the many palettes stacked around the room. Janine stood beside him as Craig searched through the piles of books. Wilbur took her hand and patted it softly. "I'm so sorry to hear what has happened, my dear. Life can be painful, but in time, you will heal."

Janine nodded and continued to cry softly. It had been difficult to look at that picture and think of how happy they had been such a short time before. She tucked it in her bag for safekeeping, placing it where she was certain it would not be damaged. Someday, she might be able to look at it again without crying. Old Wilbur was right, in time she would heal.

She talked with Wilbur about the grandfather she had never really known as Craig glanced half-heartedly through the books. She could tell that he, too, had already decided that Wilbur was not involved. That left only one other store that could be, and that would be where they headed next.

"Your grand-pop was a good man, Janine," Wilbur told her in his reedy voice. "He loved his bookstore. It was the most important thing in the world to him next to his wife and son."

"I love it, too." Janine told him with a small smile. "I'll be taking the business over shortly, and I'll make it even better than it is now. That's a promise."

"It's nice that your grand-pop's love for books has survived to your generation. It would make him proud to know that you were carrying on his legacy. He was so proud of you."

"Hopefully, I can continue to make him proud." Janine gave Wilbur a small hug as Craig walked toward them.

"Thanks for your time, Mr. Munchauser. We hope we didn't intrude on your day too much." Craig shook the man's hand, and he led them back to the door."

"Oh, no, not at all. I can always use a little excitement around here." He hugged Janine gently as Craig opened the door. "Sorry for your loss, little Neeny. It was nice to see you. Your grand-pop would be proud of the woman you've become. Take care now."

He waved them off, and Janine felt her eyes gloss over with tears again. "What a nice man," she said to Craig, taking his hand as they walked back to the Mustang. "I'm glad he wasn't involved. It's nice to know there are still good people in the world. I'd almost forgotten that lately." His kind words had perked her spirit up again.

"Me, too." Craig told her, opening her door. "Well, one more store to go."

Janine glanced at him as he sat in his seat. "I think you're right, Craig. I'm sure that Low Price Adventures is the one. It's got to be."

A short drive later, and they were there. Janine, like her father had been, was struck by the plainness of the store.

"It seems to me that if a store had been in business for more than fifty years, the outside might show a little personality. There's nothing. It could be a garage for all the decorations." Janine shook her head. "Obviously these people don't take as much pride in their store as my family always has."

Craig nodded distractedly. He pulled his cell phone out of the glove box, and swore. "Battery's dead. I can't believe I forgot to pick up a charger." He tossed the phone into the back seat unceremoniously. "How's yours?"

Janine dug through her bag until she discovered it, and shook her head. "Dead."

"We won't be able to tell the captain where we're at, then. I don't like that. So for now, we'll watch the building for a while and see if anything seems suspicious, then we'll check out the inside."

"Sounds like a plan. I've never been on a stake-out. Should be interesting." Janine unsnapped her seatbelt and crossed her legs under her, settling in.

Two hours later, Janine realized that not only was a stake-out not interesting, but it was the most positively un-interesting thing she'd ever participated in. Whatever had possessed Craig to share so many of his thoughts with her earlier had shifted, and he had sat there in the driver's seat without speaking a word the entire time, despite her various attempts at conversation.

"All right," she said. "I have never been so bored in my life. Can we go in now?"

Craig seemed to shake himself out of a trance, then sent her a small smile. "I suppose. I haven't seen anything out of the ordinary. We're only going in to look around, though. This time I want to get a warrant to search the storeroom so the case doesn't get thrown out. So we'll check it out briefly, then we'll need to inform the captain."

"Ten-four," Janine answered with a shaky smile. Suddenly she was feeling very nervous.

They walked into the store hand and hand as if they hadn't a care in the world. As any customers would do, they roamed the store, checking out various sections, and taking everything in.

Xavier watched them from behind her counter like a spider eyeing a juicy pair of flies. She'd always been able to spot a cop a mile a way, and this time was no different. Despite the shaggy excuse for a beard, she knew immediately that Detective Turner, Jr. had waltzed right into her web. The girl was harder to recognize, but logic told her it could only be Janine McMillan walking hand and hand with her bodyguard. Discreetly, she pushed a small button under the counter and instructed her men to make their way quietly to the mystery section.

"Good afternoon, folks!" She greeted them, all sugar and spice and everything nice. She wandered over to where they stood, fake smile plastered across her face. "Can I help you find anything?"

"Oh, no thanks. We're just looking." Janine replied with a similarly false smile.

Xavier paused in front of them, distracting them as she saw her men slither into the room, red handkerchiefs in hand. "I haven't seen you folks around here before. What brings you into my neck of the woods?"

Janine opened her mouth to reply, and saw a flash of red before a cloth was pressed over her mouth and nose. She tensed, preparing to defend herself as any black belt achiever would do, but an incredibly strong arm wrapped around her, pinning her arms to her sides. She had one brief moment to glimpse Craig struggling against his own attacker and to draw her leg up to kick behind her…then she drifted away into the dark, immersed in chemically scented oblivion.

Smiling, Xavier watched as her men carried them away. Whistling to herself, she turned the 'closed' sign. This seemed like an excellent time for a lunch break.

Chapter Thirteen

Janine thought she was awake, but she couldn't tell. Everything was dark. She had a nasty headache, but otherwise, it seemed that she was fully intact. It took her a moment to realize that she was blindfolded.

She jerked, and heard the screech of a wooden chair on concrete. Her hands were tied behind her back so tightly, that she had lost the feeling in her fingers. Her senses went on high alert. The room smelled damp, but still carried the lingering scent of books, so they hadn't traveled far. "Craig?" She called, startled by the creaky sound of her voice. There was no answer. "Craig!" She shouted, suddenly very afraid. An excruciatingly long minute passed until she heard him groan from directly behind her. "Are you okay?"

He moaned again, then answered in a voice as groggy as her own. "I hate chloroform. I've got one hell of a headache, but I'm fine. Are you hurt?"

"No, but I can't feel my hands."

"Shake them around a little." He felt his chair shake as she complied. "We're obviously tied together." Dimly, he became more aware of their surroundings. "I think we're alone for now, Janine." He stamped his foot only because he couldn't hit himself. "How could I have been so stupid? We could have found a pay phone and called the captain. At least then we'd have some back-up on the way."

"Don't beat yourself up, Craig, it's too late to change anything now. I'm just glad we got to wake up. We could have been dead already."

"We've got to get out of this. I doubt we have a whole lot of time. If Xavier isn't already here, I'm sure he's on his way now." Quickly, he instructed Janine in the art of loosening knots, without making it obvious. "Can you feel your hands now?"

"Yeah, they're coming back. I'll do my best." She fell silent as she concentrated on feeling the knots tied around their wrists. Biting her lip, she struggled to loosen them. Not even a minute later, she heard a door open, and quickly subsided.

"Well, well, well," said a woman's sweet, syrupy voice, "look who's awake."

None too gently, the blindfold was removed. Janine blinked. They were in a small, brightly lit office off of the storeroom in the back. The single desk was fairly tidy, adorned only with a gold-plated nameplate that read 'Alice X. Price.' Janine's gaze flew to the woman's face, and met a pair of pale brown eyes that were hard as steel behind the bifocals. "The 'X' stands for Xavier."

"Smart girl," Xavier smiled evilly. "Welcome to Low Price Adventures."

"But…," Janine stuttered, "my father referred to you as 'he.'"

"A wonderful invention called a voice distorter, my dear. Up until a couple of days ago, your father had never made my acquaintance. Needless to say, he has now."

Janine felt her heart clench. So he was dead. She struggled to feel some sorrow, but found that all she felt was emptiness. "You killed him," she said it matter-of-factly.

"Oh, no, my dear child. I'm saving him for last. First he'll have the pleasure of watching you die."

"Try it, Xavier," Craig growled.

"And your handsome friend." She sent Craig a sugary smile, then held up the guns she had taken from them. "You certainly won't be needing these." Purely to taunt them, she laid their guns on her desk.

She shifted her focus to Craig. He glared back at her as if daring her to make a move. "Young Mr. Turner." Her beady gaze skimmed over his body from head to foot and back again. "So much like your father." She felt a twinge of satisfaction as she saw him stiffen. "Oh, yes, I had the pleasure of knowing your father." Her moment to gloat had come. She strode back to her desk and settled her ample behind into her black recliner. Still grinning, she twiddled her thumbs.

"A driven man, Detective James Turner. Very dedicated to his job." She sipped from the glass of tea she had brought in with her. "I worked very closely with him for several months, purposely giving him false information that had him going in circles. He was a very trusting man. I'm afraid that was his downfall."

Craig called her a vulgar name, and struggled against his ropes. His entire body was filling with rage, all his pent-up anger rising to the surface like a volcano that has long been dormant. He could envision himself wringing his hands around that double-chinned neck and squeezing until the smugness evaporated from her dead eyes.

Mentally counting to ten, he forced himself to calm down enough to continue working at the ropes that bound him so he could do just that. He felt Janine's fingers start moving as well.

Oblivious to the increased movement, Xavier continued on. She was glad to have a new audience with which to share one of her greatest success stories. "He never even suspected that I was involved. I'm afraid he was a bit dim as well." She smirked at Craig's glare. "I remember the shock on his face when I aimed that gun at him. Before he had even realized what had happened, he was dead." She clucked her tongue. "Such a shame. And now, I have the pleasure of killing his son as well. Lucky me."

Like the press of a button, her mood changed from playful to furious as she pulled her own gun out from under her suit coat. She pointed it at Craig. "Who did you tell about this place?"

They stared back at her blankly.

Marching up to them, she pressed the muzzle of the gun to Craig's temple. "Who did you tell?" Still no answer. "Are your friends from the police department on their way?"

Craig simply glared at her.

"Perhaps you don't value your life very much, Mr. Turner. Perhaps you value hers a little more? Hmmm?" With a contemptuous grin, she pressed the gun to Janine's head instead. Pleased, she caught the fear in his eyes. He loved the girl. How precious. Sadistically, she flipped off the safety with a resounding click.

Craig averted his eyes as he saw Janine flinch. He could play with his own life, but he certainly wouldn't play with hers. "No one," he mumbled.

"Ahhh." Xavier pulled the gun away from Janine's temple and strode back to her desk. "And why not? Don't you believe in teamwork, Mr. Turner?"

"We weren't able to reach anyone."

Once again, she clucked her tongue. "Oh, that's too bad. No one on the way to rescue you. Such a pity."

She rose from her chair and paced the room. Confident that her captives were going nowhere, she placed her gun back inside her coat and changed the subject. "Yours is a persistent family, Detective. No one else has ever come so close to discovering my true identity." She paused and aimed a glare filled with hatred in his direction. Her voice became dangerously low. "*No one.*" She pounded her fist on her desk for emphasis. "For that, you must pay."

Her round face contorted with rage, she turned to face them once again. "For over thirty years I have run this business without any interference from the police. I built it from the ground up and carried it until it was a multi-million dollar industry. James Turner was so easy to manipulate, that he had no chance of discovering the truth. So I toyed with him until I was ready to eliminate him. Then *you* come along and almost ruin everything!"

She pointed to Janine. "And you! Meddling in your father's affairs like any spoiled brat would do. If you had kept your nose buried in your schoolbooks, my dear, none of this would have happened. If your father wasn't so dimwitted and weak, things never would have gotten this far!"

Suddenly Xavier seemed to calm. "To think that I, Alice Xavier Price, was actually nervous that you would destroy everything that I had built..." She laughed a short, staccato laugh of disbelief. "I'm much too smart for all of you. I didn't even have to find you. You walked right into my store like cows to the slaughter! I needed only to have been a little more patient." Leaning against her desk, she smiled wickedly, and suddenly, her face was all business as she once again took out her gun. "Now I'll toy with you before I kill you simply because I can. Miss McMillan, I believe I have someone here that would *love* to see you."

"Armando! Manuel!" She bellowed suddenly, causing both Craig and Janine to jump, afraid that she had noticed they'd almost loosened the ropes.

Before she'd recovered, Janine received a second shock upon the sight of her father. He was battered and bruised, bent over as if his ribs were broken, as they probably were. His hands were bound as well, and he could barely walk. She felt a stirring of pity at what he'd been through. Xavier's men tossed him on the floor as if he were no more than a sack of flour. Despite his injuries, her feelings toward him had changed forever. She barely acknowledged his cry of greeting.

"Neeny! Baby!" Ray cried, tears streaming from his eyes, utterly devastated to find her here. He turned angry eyes on Craig. "How could you lead her here? You were supposed to protect her! Now look what you've done!"

"What I've done doesn't even come close to what you've done, McMillan." Craig glared at him with equal contempt.

"Enough!" Xavier cried. "Gentlemen," she said to her guards, "let's show Miss McMillan just how much we appreciate what her father's done for us."

The huge bodyguards grinned with wicked excitement, and set to work beating Ray to a bloody pulp once again.

Janine closed her eyes, unable to watch, and wished that she could shut her ears as well to block out her father's howls of pain. Shutting her mind off, she turned her focus back to the ropes until finally, she felt them loosen. She flicked Craig, hoping that he would understand what she was telling him. When he flicked her back, all they had to do was wait for the right moment.

The moment was quick to come.

At the snap of Xavier's fingers, the bodyguards ceased their assault on Ray and stood at attention. Ray released one final gasp of pain, and slumped to the ground, his breath heaving. His blue eyes were filled with pain as he stared at Janine, pleading silently for help.

Xavier smiled her evil smile, and turned to grab her tea.

Craig knew that this might be the only chance they'd get. With a war cry, he stood, grabbing the chair and flinging it at the unsuspecting bodyguards. They stumbled back in surprise and ducked for cover. Janine quickly followed his lead, aiming her own chair at the back of Xavier's head. She missed, but the impact of the chair on Xavier's back knocked the woman to the ground just long enough.

Craig dove for their guns, praying that they were still loaded. As Xavier began to heave herself up, he had them in his hands. He tossed Janine her gun, ordering her to find cover. She whipped behind a palette in the back of the room, checking her gun as she went. It was still loaded. She saw her father lying on the floor near her, and without a thought for her own safety she dragged him behind the palette with her. There was no sense in letting him die before he made it to prison.

"Oh, God. Thank you, Neeny!" Ray cried.

"Shut up." Janine told him fiercely, focusing on Craig.

She watched as he flew behind the palette nearest him, heard him gasp as she watched a bullet pierce his side. The bodyguards had regained their ground and were coming after him full force. Peering around from the corner, he fired back, nicking one on the shoulder, and knocking the gun out of the other one's hands. A bullet pierced the corner of the palette, and a flood of white powder coated the floor. There was his proof. An instant later, one of the bodyguards fell, his heart pierced by Craig's bullet.

A movement on the other side of the room caught Janine's eye. Xavier had circled the room and was approaching Craig from behind, gun drawn and a maniacal grin on her face.

Janine took aim, all of her concentration focused on hitting her target. She squeezed the trigger and watched as her bullet smacked into the wall directly in front of Xavier.

Xavier cried out as a fountain of stone burst from the wall in front of her nose. The girl was shooting at her! "Get her!" Xavier called to her one remaining bodyguard, kicking herself for allowing her defenses to dwindle to two incompetent bodyguards on the home front.

Unaware of what was going on around him, Craig only saw the bodyguard turn in Janine's direction. He watched in agony as the man squeezed off a shot.

Click. It seemed to echo off the walls all around the office, reverberating like a timpani drum.

The breath whooshed out of Craig's lungs. The gorilla's gun was empty. Knowing that he only had one shot left, Craig took aim.

Janine stood her ground as the bodyguard rushed her. She knew she had only seconds left. She had to make this shot count. Once again she focused, clearing everything from her mind except Xavier's beady little eyes as the woman aimed her gun at Craig. Praying that she wouldn't miss, Janine squeezed off a shot just as a huge mountain of man and muscle slammed into her.

Craig jumped at Janine's shot. What had she been aiming at? His heart lurching in his chest, he turned and looked behind him. He jumped as he looked down at Xavier's body, her smile still in place, her gun pointed directly at him.

And a wicked looking hole right between her eyes.

Without another thought, Craig raced to Janine's aid where she and the bodyguard were fighting over possession of the one remaining gun, Janine using her black belt karate to the best of her ability. Craig thundered to a stop behind the man and shot him point blank in the temple without hesitation.

Armando or Manuel fell to the floor with a thump, and the room fell silent.

Chapter Fourteen

Barely, Craig avoided a well aimed high-kick to the head.
Janine gasped, and drew back at just the right moment.
They stared at each other for a moment, and burst into laughter at the stunned look on each other's faces. Laughing like loons, they dropped to the floor.
"You almost killed me!" Craig gave a big belly laugh of astonishment, and groaned as the pain in his side flared. Almost as quickly as it had started, the laughter stopped
"Oh my God!" Janine cried, "You're hurt!" She flung herself on him, hands groping everywhere to see if he had any more injuries.
"Stop! Stop! I'm okay! It's just a flesh wound!" Unconcerned with the blood on his hands, he grasped Janine's face. "I'm okay."
She mirrored the gesture, and for a moment they gazed into each other's eyes as if to confirm that they were both still whole.
The fear that he had clamped down on during the entire shootout overwhelmed Craig, and he took her mouth in a rough, possessive kiss. The taste of her soothed his tattered nerves, and he pulled her closer.
Janine wrapped her arms around him, putting all of her heart and soul into the meeting of mouths, wallowing in the need that flowed from him in waves.
He hugged her to him as if trying to pull her inside of him where she would be safe. When the thought of what could have happened

finally faded from his mind, he released her lips, pressing his face into her hair.

The simple embrace meant more to Janine than a thousand of the most passionate kisses. She allowed herself to be comforted by his warmth, her eyes growing damp with tears as she realized the sweetness of it.

"I love you, Janine," Craig spoke softly into her ear, his hand caressing her hair.

When Janine heard him speak the words that she'd been longing to hear her heart burst with happiness. Despite all that had happened, she had found love. In a choked voice, she responded, "I love you, Craig."

Craig felt warmth flow through him. He had found someone he could spend the rest of his life with...when he finally got his life back together. There were a few things he needed to take care of yet before they took that step. For now, he simply held her as if he never wanted to let her go.

The moment was broken by the sound of sniffling coming from somewhere behind them. They broke apart, startled to find that they were not alone in the room.

Ray gazed at them with tears in his blackened eyes, holding his bound hands to his heart as if to keep it from flying from his chest. He smiled at them softly, revealing a few missing teeth to compliment the bruises. "I'm so happy for you, Neeny." He spoke in a voice rough with tears. For the moment, he was the father she remembered. "At least something good came from all of this. I know he'll take care of you." He turned his gaze on Craig with a lopsided, split-lipped grin of approval. "He's a good man. Better than I ever was."

"Thank you," was Janine's response, spoken without a hint of warmth.

"Thank you for saving my life," Ray said quietly.

"Saving your life is the last thing I'll ever do for you, Ray. From this point on, I have no father. You're dead to me." She didn't even react as her father flinched.

Craig rose, offered Janine his hand. "Let's find a phone and call the captain. We'll see how many more of Xavier's goons we can round up by the end of the day."

She took his hand and, turning her back on Ray, followed him to the desk.

"No matter what happens now or in the future, Neeny," Ray called after them, both tears and acceptance in his voice. "I want you to know that I'm so proud that I raised such a strong and intelligent woman. Your mother would be proud too. I hope you always remember that. And I hope that somewhere, deep down inside, you'll remember that you loved me once, and I hope you know that even if I never see you again, I'll always love you. Always." With a sob and a sigh, Ray fell silent as he watched his daughter walk away from him for the last time, thankful that at least she had heard what he had wanted to say.

A short distance away, Krista Mulroney hung up the phone and breathed a sigh of relief. It was finally over. She took her keys out of her pocket and swung them around, trying to decide if she should let her husband continue to rot in his cell for a while, or let him loose.

As much as some twisted part of her wanted to leave him there for a week or two, she had to admit to herself that she missed him. With a purposeful stride, she marched over to the jail.

Mark looked awful. He sat on the stone bench, his face in his hands, his once pressed suit ragged and filthy. She rattled her keys as she dug for the right one, silently thankful that he hadn't had to put up with a roommate while he'd been in there. That could have traumatized him beyond repair.

Mark heard the jingling and glanced up. His wife had never looked as wonderful to him as she did right now. He was at the bars in a flash, ready to go home. "You caught him?"

She nodded. "He's safe, as are Detective Turner and his daughter."

"Thank God. I don't know what I would have done if something had happened to them."

"You would have sat in prison for the next several years." He blanched at her terse response. Despite herself, a small grin tugged at her lips. "I'm letting you out of here on two conditions, Mulroney."

"Anything you want, I'll do it."

"Promise me that you'll never go behind my back like that again."

"I promise. What's the second condition?"

"When we get home," she stepped closer, then wrinkled her nose at the stench of him, "*after* you shower, you're going to do absolutely anything I want you to do." She sent him a slightly wicked glance, her eyes twinkling. "You've got a lot of time to make up for."

Mark laughed. "It'll be my pleasure."

She unlocked the door, and was quickly wrapped in his embrace. She wrapped her arms around him and hugged him back. Despite the nasty smell, it felt good simply to have him hold her again. She let herself enjoy it for a moment, then briskly stepped back.

"Hit the showers, Mulroney," she ordered. "I'll see you at home." With a wink, she marched back to her desk. She had a drug ring to take care of.

A week later, the police had managed to round up everyone who had been involved in the smuggling, and were working on forming a client list. Thanks to Alice Xavier Price's orderly, librarian files, the task had not been difficult.

Ray McMillan's injuries had been tended to, and he was currently residing in the county jail until his trial, after which he would probably spend the rest of his life in Stillwater Penitentiary.

After the dust had settled, Craig found himself standing outside the blue house with white shutters that he had shared with his wife in North Minneapolis so long ago. It looked almost exactly the same. The bushes and flowers were bigger and brighter now, and Karen had put up a white picket fence around the front yard. The paint on the house was fresh, giving it a cheerful appearance.

Craig stared at the front door for a while, awash in memories of the good old days before his father had been killed. He and Karen had been happy together once, that he knew for sure. He knew that she had remarried now, though he didn't even know the name of her new husband. He hadn't even seen her for thirteen years. She had found someone that was better for her than him, just as he had found Janine.

Squaring his shoulders, Craig marched up the steps and rang the doorbell.

When Karen answered the door, peering at him through the screen, he simply stood there and smiled at her for a moment. She looked the same as well, though slightly older. Her shoulder-length brown hair was curled under at the ends, accenting her heart-shaped face. Her eyes were the same green, of course, though decorated at the corners with the beginning of laugh lines. It made him happy to see those, to know that despite what he'd put her through, she had been happy enough to laugh often. The expression on her face was pure shock.

"Craig? What are you doing here?" She made no move to open the door.

"It's good to see you, Karen. You look good." He nodded.

"Thank you. You look pretty good yourself."

"Would you sit on the step with me for a while? I don't need to come in, but I'd like to talk to you." He saw the doubt in her eyes briefly before she covered it up with a polite smile.

"Sure." She opened the door and stepped out, and he noticed the bulge of her belly.

"Pregnant again, huh?" he asked, settling beside her on the step.

"I remarried, as I'm sure you know. This will be the second child that Tom and I have had together. Ethan has a sister that's four." Her back was stiff, and it was very obvious that she wasn't very comfortable talking to him.

"Congratulations, Karen. I'm happy for you."

She relaxed a little. "Thanks. What have you been up to?"

Craig took a deep breath. "I'm happy for the first time in thirteen years."

A flash of the old Karen broke through as she grabbed his shoulder.

"You found him? The one that killed your father?"

He patted her hand. "Yep. Turned out that it was a woman." He told her the whole story as quickly as he could. "So now I'm finally ready to take back control of my life."

"That's wonderful, Craig. I'm happy for you."

He turned to face her, took her hand, glad when she didn't pull away. "I came here today to tell you that I'm sorry about what I put you through. I'm sorry that I was so focused on my father's death that I let you and Ethan slip away. It was the biggest mistake I ever made."

A tear slipped down her cheek, but she brushed it away. "Thank you. That's nice to hear." She took her own deep breath. "Ethan's here if you'd like to meet him."

"Would you let me?" At her nod, Craig breathed a sigh of relief. "I know he probably won't like me now, but I'd like to start fixing that."

"I'm glad you want to try. I'll send him out. I really am happy for you, and I hope that you're happy with Janine. I hope that both of you will be involved in Ethan's life from now on."

"Thanks, Karen. You take care." He watched her walk in the house, and stood up to pace. He was nervous. His hands were shaking and his heart was thumping. What if his own son didn't like him? What if he couldn't forgive him for walking out before he was born? He only had a few moments to fret before the door opened behind him.

When he turned to look at the boy that walked outside, Craig was taken aback by how much of himself he could see in his son. Ethan had the same shaggy, wavy brown hair, cut almost the same as his own, Craig's brown eyes, and even the same rough and ready stance. Ethan was like a miniature version of himself, though there was a little of Karen in his bone structure and attitude. For a moment Craig was stunned to silence as he felt love wash over him.

"Hey," Ethan said quietly, tucking his thumbs in the front pockets of his jeans and eyeing Craig warily.

"Hey, Ethan. It's nice to meet you." Craig stuck out his hand, and was impressed by the boy's firm handshake. "You've got a good grip. Tough kid."

A small smile bloomed on his son's face. "Thanks. I'm going to be a cop, just like you and grandpa."

They sat on the front step together and talked for more than an hour. Craig was surprised at how easy it was to talk to this son he'd never met, and how easily Ethan had accepted him. It had almost seemed as if Ethan had been waiting for the day to come when he would meet his father, though he loved his stepfather very much. By the end of their visit, they had made plans to go to a Viking's game together in the fall. Apparently, Ethan was a big fan. When Craig left, he offered his son his hand again, and was touched when the boy held his arms out for a hug.

Craig's heart melted as he embraced the boy. "I'm sorry it took me so long to meet you, Ethan. I've thought about you a lot over the years."

Ethan patted his back and stepped back, with a very adult look in his eyes. "That's okay…Dad. You weren't ready. I'm glad you are now."

"Me, too. See you around, tough guy." With a huge smile on his face, Craig waved and walked back to his Mustang. He fully intended to make up for all the time he'd missed of being a father. Now that he was back in control of his life, he planned to enjoy every single minute of it. All he had left to do to complete his new beginning was to get himself the girl.

Janine's life had returned somewhat to normal. She had taken over the bookstore, fully expecting to be closing it for awhile. To her surprise, as soon as the story had gotten out, the bookstore's business had doubled. She knew that it was only temporary and that things would settle down, but for now, it was keeping her busy, especially since she needed to hire all new help.

Her father's money had all been confiscated, Swiss bank accounts included, and Janine was very thankful that she had some money saved of her own. She had put the house that she had grown up in on the market, and since she had not found a place to live yet, she was hoping that it wouldn't sell too quickly.

For now, she was enjoying being back where she belonged. Despite all that had happened, she still loved the bookstore, and she looked forward to making it her own. She walked down the sidewalk toward her father's home, feeling almost happy for the first time in a long time. She tipped her face to the June sunshine, enjoying the feel of the gentle breeze on the back of her neck, a sensation she had rarely felt when her hair had been long.

When the silver mustang screeched to the curb beside her, Janine was momentarily taken aback to when everything had started. Only this time, the car stopped and the man she loved stepped out with an enormous smile on his face.

Craig picked Janine up and swung her around, hugging her tightly. When he stopped spinning, he lowered her just enough so he could take her lips in a heart-stopping kiss.

Janine's mind went momentarily blank as she was overwhelmed by the feelings he brought out in her, the deepest of which was love. She felt as if she was still floating when her feet touched the ground. Keeping her arms around his waist, she asked him, "What was that for?"

"My life is finally just how I want it to be." He grinned at her. "I saw Karen and Ethan today. Ethan's great. I can't believe I missed out on so much of his life. He's just like me. Makes me want to have a few more children. Do you like children?"

"Sure, I do, but..." her words were cut off when he kissed her again.

"Good, because when we're married I want to have at least two or three more."

Janine held a hand to her spinning head. "When we're married?"

He pulled a box out of his pocket and flipped the lid. Diamonds twinkled at her as if they were filled with the light of the sun. "Will you marry me, Janine?"

For a moment she was stunned. Then she felt happiness spread from the tips of her toes to the top of her head, mingled with pure excitement that she could keep this wonderful man. "Of course I will!" She cried, jumping into his arms. "I love you so much!"

"I love you right back, Janine. I promise I'll take care of you and never let anything happen to you again." He kissed her again, this woman that he had fallen in love with so quickly. The woman he would marry and have children with, begin a whole new happier life with.

The sun sparkled down on them, the sky was clear and bright, the world was beautiful, and her whole future was ahead of her. It was a new beginning for the new Janine. She would begin this new life with the love of a strong man and her newly acquired knowledge of her own strength, her own power, and her ability to love with absolutely no illusions.